Volume Nine

Airship 27 Productions

Sinbad the New Voyages Volume 9

Published by Airship 27 Productions
www.airship27.com
www.airship27hangar.com

Editor: Ron Fortier
Associate Editor: Gordon Dymowski
Marketing and Promotions Manager: Michael Vance
Art Director/Designer: Rob Davis

ISBN: 978-1-969285-15-8

Produced in the United States of America

10 9 8 7 6 5 4 3 2 1

Volume Nine Contents

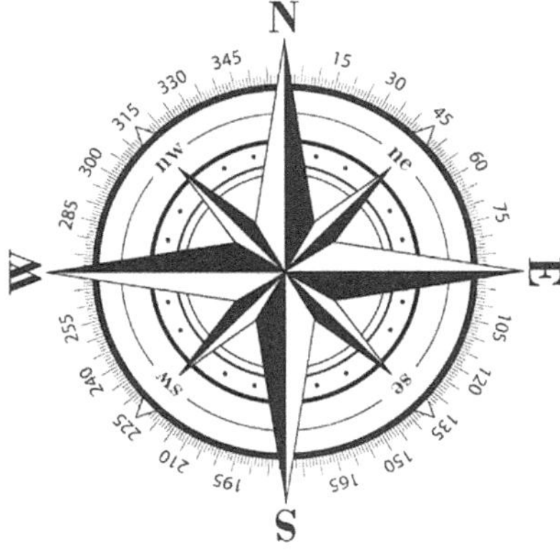

Sinbad and the Forbidden City

by Richard C. White

The storyteller waved the crowd closer to the fire as the caravan settled in for the evening. A cool wind blew in from the desert making the tent flaps move in time with the flickering flames. There was a soft murmur from the surrounding caravan guards and drivers, each showing the wear of the journey in their clothing and their faces. The camels made contented noises where they were tethered in the lee of a sand dune, as protected from the elements as they could be in this terrain.

The moon rose on the horizon, and served to spotlight the storyteller as he rose to his feet and addressed the assembled crowd. "Allah be praised my friends; we have traveled far today. With some luck, the spires of Baghdad will soon rise before us like a beacon guiding a lonely ship to port. Still, we are but one humble caravan. Just pilgrims passing through this life until we reach the glories of the afterlife."

He paused to ensure everyone was watching before continuing. "Ah, but you don't want to hear stories about people like us, told and retold over countless treks through this desert. No, tonight, let me tell you a story about one of the greatest seamen to ever sail the seven seas. One blessed by the heavens to survive and thrive in situations that would make a poor mortal quail, and a brave man curl up in fear. I speak of none other than Sinbad, the most famous sailor ever to live."

"We have heard the tales, Malik. We can almost quote the stories of his seven voyages as well as you," one of the guards scoffed. "Has not the beautiful Shahrazad told all there is to know about this man?"

"I would never try to usurp the fair Shahrazad's place in the realm of master storytellers, Casmir," Malik said, raising his hands to illustrate no ill intent. "I am but a poor humble man who earns a meager living from his tales, but yes. I believe I have learned a tale not in that fair maiden's repertoire. So, if you'll gather closer, you may learn something new about the Sinbad, and…

Malik paused artfully, then brought his hands down to indicate the small blanket set before him. "Perhaps if you find my story entertaining enough, a few coins for my efforts might be compensation for my poor voice."

"Where's the compensation for our ears?" Casmir laughed but tossed a few dinar onto the blanket. "For your poor voice, *sahib*"

"The blessings of Allah upon you, good Casmir. Now, this was several years ago. The *Blue Nymph* had just reached the port of Basrah after another successful voyage…"

"Captain!" the curly-haired look-out called down from his accustomed spot at the top of the mast. "How long are we going to be in port this time?"

Sinbad stood at the rail next to the gangplank, staring at the docks. No matter how many times the *Blue Nymph* sailed into Basrah, he never tired of the hustle and bustle. Day workers were already lining up to off-load whatever extraordinary cargo the famed Sinbad would be delivering on this day.

"Hard to say, Haroun," he replied. "Only Allah deals in absolutes. We mere mortals must adapt to whatever the Almighty decides to send our way." He paused before he laughed and then spoke again with a smile on his face. "Or at least, that's what the imam would say if you asked him. I intend to sail in a week's time, or sooner if we can find a fine cargo to transport."

A large shadow fell on Sinbad and he turned to see Ralf Gunarson towering over him. The Northman ran his fingers through his blonde beard and sniffed the air. "Captain, no offense to anyone on this ship, but take your time. I intend to enjoy sampling every restaurant and inn's menu and eating to my heart's fill. Jelal knows several dozen fish recipes, but man was not meant to live on fish alone. I need good red meat and something to wash it down."

"Patience, my friend. Business first and then we will certainly see what can be found in Basrah once the sun goes down." He laughed and clasped the giant man's shoulder before speaking softer. "I too have grown weary of fish and fowl, but I am the captain. Is it not right that I share the men's food with them?

Sinbad almost started as a soft, but powerful woman's voice sounded behind him. "I personally am quite pleased with fish and fowl, Captain, although, the manner in how it is served some nights makes me question my choices in life."

"Tishimi, by Allah, woman, you move like a shadow. Had you not spoken, I wouldn't have known you were there."

The lithe Japanese woman stood behind him, her arms crossed over her chest, weapons omnipresent as usual. "Your insensitive ears are not my fault, Captain," she observed mildly.

"Be that as it may, I try to cater to your needs, but not everyone likes eating their fish raw."

"I do not object to cooked fish, per se. Just some of the manners in which it is cooked."

Ralf nudged Sinbad. "She speaks? The food must have been really bad this trip."

Tishimi's expression didn't change as she turned her eyes upward at her hulking companion. "I had something to add to the conversation. Having said it, I will withdraw."

"Will you be going ashore, Tishimi?" Sinbad said, taking advantage of her presence. It was rare for Tishimi to engage in conversation unrelated to battle or the ship's activities.

The *onna-musha* paused before nodding slowly. "I am running low on ink, and I desire some new pen nibs. I am working on something I would like to finish before we make port the next time. Given the chaos that follows you, better to secure the items I need now rather than rely on chance."

Before Sinbad could say anything more, Tishimi gave a small bow and left. The crew parted as she made her way aft and soon disappeared in the direction of the stern. A soft whistle came from nearby and Omar made his way over to Sinbad, a long piece of paper in his hand.

The gray-haired man muscled his way past a couple of slower sailors to reach Sinbad's side. "Captain, here is the inventory of the cargo. If you'll please sign off, I'll get the laborers to carry them to the usual warehouse. I see Salim on the dock, which means he's ready to take them until he can find buyers."

"Ah, Omar, what would I do without you? While I am here, wool-gathering with my companions, you're hard at work. Why, some might say this is more your ship than mine."

"And they'd be fools. I am your first mate and my purpose in life is to ensure the captain does not have to worry about small things." There was a motion at the man's feet and a gray streak of fur appeared, intertwining itself between Omar's legs. Once Omar had stopped talking and looked down at him. Samson dropped a large rat at his feet and then sat down looking quite pleased with himself.

"If it isn't the infinite stomach. I swear, cat, you eat more than seven djinns. Allah tests me daily with your presence. It's my own fault thought for being so kind-hearted. Go now, take your prize to Jalal and he will give you a reward for your bravery."

The cat glared at the human almost as if he understood the burly first mate, meowed, and picked up the rat and pranced off with his prize.

Ralf guffawed as the cat walked away. "Oh ho, Sinbad. I believe there walks away the real master of this ship."

"We'll discuss this mutinous talk later, over some cups, Ralf. No, Omar is right, we need to get this ship unloaded and see to supplies and repairs. Then, and only then, can we take time to enjoy ourselves, but enjoy ourselves we will."

Evening in Basrah found the crew of the *Blue Nymph* enjoying the smells and sounds of a tavern several blocks away from the docks. Here sailors from every nation mingled, swapping stories and making deals. Sinbad and his friends had taken a table in a corner in the back and were listening to the musicians performing on the stage as the servers brought out plate after plate of fresh food and vegetables.

Sinbad glanced over and spotted one of his men sitting upright, alert and spying the crowd with a wary eye. "Henri, can you not relax? This is Basrah, our home port."

The Gaul ran a hand through his brown hair and stared out over the crowd. Always the pessimist, he adjusted his tunic which Sinbad knew hid his leathers beneath. "Yes, this is Basrah, and while you are a forgiving and generous man, there are those in this port who are neither. After all, we've all had our narrow brushes with death in these streets. I just think it prudent to pay attention to what's going on around us tonight."

"Who would want to harm me, Henri?"

The Gaul looked over at him and deadpanned, "How many hours do you have? I can safely say that for every porter, longshoreman, merchant and noble who consider you a friend, I can name almost the same number of merchants and nobles whom you've crossed swords with at one time or another. My friend, you take more chances than one should, and I say this as a master of games of chance."

"But, Henri, what is life without adventure? And I have never drawn a weapon on one who did not deserve it. I am no simple thief, and I have never cheated a man in a deal save when he tried to cheat me first. No, if someone has enmity with me then it is on their head, not mine. I go where Allah's winds take me and sip deeply from the wine of life."

"Still, a little caution from time to time is not a bad thing."

Sinbad waved a hand at his friend and turned back to the rest of his companions at the table. Most were rapturously watching the dancing girls who were performing with the musicians, and he found himself paying close attention to one of the dancers. His dark blue eyes took in her beauty, and it took him a few minutes to realize the musicians had stopped playing. He jerked himself upright as a large man in heavily stained work clothes made his way across the tavern and stopped directly in front of Sinbad's table.

"So, you show your face in Basrah after all that has happened?"

Sinbad stared up at the red-faced man in confusion. "I am sorry, my friend, but you are unfamiliar to me."

"Dog, you ruin me and then you claim to have forgotten me? Allah protect me from fools. I am Ibrahim, the former scribe of the Vizir of Estafan. You stuck your nose in where it was not wanted and caused the Vizir to fall, taking me down with him. For years, I have worked on the docks! My hands that once wrote missives to the powerful and influential are now beaten and broken from carrying cargo, for none will hire me."

William, a Scotsman to Sinbad's right leaned heavily against the table, his scarred arms and swarthy features made almost demonic in the flickering lamplight. "Here now, who the devil are you to come over here and throw baseless accusations against our captain. If he says he doesn't know you, then he doesn't know you."

"Baseless accusations? Hold your tongue, foreigner. This is not your place to speak."

William started to rise, but Sinbad placed a hand on his arm and gently restrained him. He spread his hands and motioned for everyone else at the table to remain seated and waited until he felt the tension subside in his crew. He motioned for someone to bring up a chair for the angry man, but his antagonist refused to be seated. With as calm a voice as he could muster, Sinbad spoke to him, "My good man, Allah knows I pity your current situation, but the Vizir used foul magicks to bewitch the daughter of the Emir. That I saved her from her intended fate, I do *not* apologize for. However, if my actions against such an evil man caused you to wind up in your straits, especially if you were unaware of his intentions, then I most humbly beg your forgiveness. That was not my intent."

The man seemed confused with Sinbad's reaction, but taking a deep breath, he pressed on. "Intention or not, none will hire me because of my association with that scoundrel. Once my name is known, it is only a matter of time before I must leave or starve. I came to Basrah with the intent of seeking you out to secure the justice I deserve."

Omar broke in before Sinbad could stop him. "Justice . . . or revenge?"

"Whichever Allah will grant me," the man said, but he paused again, almost as if Sinbad's contrition had reached him. "However, it is true that not every egress requires blood to be shed to receive justice."

Sinbad considered the man standing in front of him. He was a proud one, but Sinbad did not see the taint of evil his patron had. Omar looked at him, but Sinbad shook his head. He knew offering this man money would only enflame his pride more and push things to a breaking point. He thought a bit more then motioned for the man to sit.

"You come to me with an honest complaint and never let it be said that Sinbad, son of the sea, ever left an honest man in the lurch. Come to the *Blue Nymph* in the morning, and I will introduce you to a friend. He is a merchant of means and has many warehouses. A man of your talents should help him ensure his business runs smoothly. It may not be as grand a position as the one you left in Estafan, but it will be honest work and, if Allah wills, it will lead to opportunities in the future."

The man collapsed into the chair, as if his muscles had been severed. "By Allah, I had come to this tavern swearing either you or I would not leave her alive, but I now see I was a fool. You are not the Sinbad I had built up in my mind over the years. My most humble apologies, *effendi.*"

"Not to worry, friend. Every act has consequences, even if we do not directly see them. Please join us for a while. Eat and drink your fill. This is the least I can do to make things right."

While the crew relaxed and turned to make the stranger welcome, Sinbad rose and made his way through the tavern. Even through the commotion at his table, he had noticed the young dancer had paused and when she had his attention had motioned to a hallway in the back of the tavern.

It could well be a trap, Sinbad, but then again . . .

He slipped into the smoke-filled hallway and saw there were several doors that he assumed led to dressing rooms for the performers and a stairway going upstairs. With no sign of the dancer in the area, he cautiously made his way to the stairwell and then began climbing. At the top was a large room, encompassing the entirety of the hallway below. It was lined with the richest of Persian rugs, both on the floor and hanging from the walls. The furniture was made of ebon wood from the west of Africa and teak from the Sind. There was a smell of incense burning from the corner. Amidst this splendor, the dancer was lounging on some pillows to his right, but another caught his eye.

She was tall and from her build, Sinbad assumed she had been a dancer once upon a time. Her flaming red hair and exotic clothing told him she was not a native of Basrah and she lifted a crystal chalice from the mahogany table she was seated at in his direction. "Ah, Sinbad, I am so glad you decided to accept Talia's invitation. I would have come to fetch you myself, but this is a matter of some . . . delicacy, so the fewer people who know about this meeting, the better."

"I'm afraid you have me at a disadvantage, miss. For a second time tonight, someone I have never met seems entirely too familiar with me."

She laughed and set another goblet on the table in front of her. "Please, it is not right we should speak to each other from across the room. Talia, please go downstairs and seek out Omar, the large, muscular man at Sinbad's table. Tell him that his captain is negotiating a new voyage and will rejoin them shortly." She threw some gold coins on the table. "Give them to Omar with my regards. Tell him, their visit is on the house and they may stay as long as they like to satisfy themselves I mean their captain no harm."

"I'm afraid you'll find Omar a hard man to convince."

"You haven't seen Talia's skills at persuasion. Now, please, Sinbad, take a seat, relax and enjoy yourself. I am Adara, the owner of this establishment and many others. We are not so different, except you seek your fortune at sea and I find my fortune here on land."

"If tonight's crowd is any indication, your fortune finds you."

"It depends on whether the fleets are in or out. But, we are not here to discuss the vagaries of business. No, my dear adventurer, I have need of your services. Services that no one else on the seven seas can provide."

"Well, if my talents are that in demand, it's a poor negotiating tactic to let me know so soon. You'll only drive my price up."

She reached down beside her chair and tossed a bag across the table to him as if she was tossing a coin to a passing beggar. The bag landed with a solid thunk and Sinbad didn't have to look to know if was heavily laden.

"You'll find I'm not in the mood to negotiate. What I seek can only be found within the next four weeks, or it will not be found again until both of us are but a memory in the desert. You have heard of Umar before?"

Sinbad tried to keep his features calm, but . . . *Umar* . . . the lost city. The rumors ran rampant in the taverns and docks regarding the fabled riches of a city cursed to sink beneath the sands, only to appear one week every hundred years. A city said to be inhabited by ghouls and divs, where the spirits of those who had sought the city and failed were doomed to spend eternity.

"You need not speak, Sinbad. Your expression says you know of what I speak. I have acquired the knowledge and the means to enter the city, but I am not skilled enough to reach it safely. You, on the other hand, are known being fearless and seeking out locations most men should not. I believe you and your crew have the skills and courage to brave the Rub al'Khali and can reach Umar while it is still accessible."

"I also know that if we do not reach it, we could easily wander the desert for the rest of our very short lives. It is called the Empty Quarter for a reason, Adara."

"Ah, but most explorers do not have this, Sinbad." She reached down beside her chair again and carefully set a sextant, a large black stone, and a rolled-up piece of paper. She carefully spread the roll open to show a map listing seasonal oases and the approximate distance between each. "This map was painstakingly created over the past ten years. My people also secured this sextant to measure the stars, and while I'm certain you have one also, this one was especially prepared by a European wizard to be unbreakable. I also secured this lodestone, which will always show the way north, so by aligning the night stars with the lodestone and then by use of the sextant, your navigator should have no issues finding the way to the unfindable city."

"You seem to have thought of everything. So why do you need me?"

She laughed again, and Sinbad found himself admiring her peri-like qualities. She looked barely old enough to be out of her father's house and yet, she spoke as one who'd seen much of the world in her lifetime. She leaned forward and smiled at Sinbad. "As I said, you have something of a reputation in Basrah. If you need the impossible to occur, there is no one else but Sinbad to call upon. Besides, even if I were to make my own way there, who knows what dangers lurk. No, I need a captain and crew who are prepared to deal with whatever the fates throw their way."

Sinbad picked up the bag and gave it a couple of quick shakes. He could tell from the sound this bag held no coins, but gems. A rakish smile crossed his lips, and he tucked the bag through his belt. "So, when do I start?"

"We."

Sinbad shook his head. "I already have a seasoned crew, as you have noted. I do not wish to add supercargo to a dangerous mission. You should remain here, and I will secure the treasure and bring it to you."

"I'm afraid you don't get to make that choice, Sinbad. The deal is for me to go with you. Oh, I forgot to tell you, there is a specific incantation one must give to enter the city with any hope of being able to leave. I'm the only one qualified to recite it." She ran her hands down her sides and smiled at him. "Besides, it will be a long trip. It might give us time to get to know one another better."

Sinbad's conscience fought with him for a moment before his roguish side won out. He lifted his glass to her in acquiescence. "A beautiful travel companion, treasure, and a story to confound people for the ages. Who could possibly say no to all that?"

She returned his salute with her own glass. "Who indeed, Sinbad? Who indeed?"

After sealing the deal with a drink, he excused himself while he still could and made his way down the stairs to rejoin his crew. As he approached the table, the crew rose to greet him and waited until he was seated before they took their places.

Haround grinned at him as he took his seat. "By Allah, I was beginning to worry about you, Sinbad. You were gone much longer than that dancer told us you would be detained."

"Let's just say, negotiations were a little more complicated than I had anticipated."

Omar dug an elbow into his ribs. "Negotiations. Hah."

"For once, you suspicious old sea dog, there were only negotiations. Besides,

I received word that your wife was looking for you at the docks. Shouldn't you go see her?"

Omar laughed, "Well, that all depends. Which one?"

Tishimi let out a disgusted noise. "How many wives do you have in Basrah?"

That comment elicited a round of laughter from the other men at the table before Omar continued. "Only one is *from* Basrah, but any of them could have come to Basrah. I won't know until I see how many kids she has in tow."

Sinbad spread his arms open, gathering the attention of everyone at the table. "My friends, I have accepted our next commission. Let us enjoy this evening because starting tomorrow, we will have a lot of work to do. I will discuss the particulars of this job tomorrow when there are fewer ears to listen in, however innocently. Still, Tishimi, I will need you to clear some room in your cabin for a second bed."

The whole crew turned to Sinbad with a disapproving eye. "And why would that be, Captain?" Henri asked, lifting an eyebrow.

"Our patron will be joining us, and I do not find it appropriate for them to sleep with the rest of the men on our ship."

Omar scoffed. "He's too important to hobnob with the rest of us?"

"*She's* too much of a woman to trust you dogs around her. Tishimi's cabin is probably the safest place for her on the entire ship," Sinbad corrected mildly.

The table became suddenly quiet, before Omar spoke up. "Now, Captain. Since we're not at sea, I hope I can speak my mind."

"As long as you mind what you say."

"I object strenuously. While I do not know what this mission entails, I know deep in my heart that this will be no place for a woma . . . Ouch."

Tishimi bowed her head slightly. "My pardons, first mate. I did not mean to kick you. I was just shifting position."

Omar shot her a dirty look and scooted his chair backward before continuing. "This will be no place for a woman who doesn't know how to fight." He finished the last part quickly, shifting to protect his shins. "I know we've had women on board before, but I still believe it's tempting fate to continue to do so."

"Omar, if Allah wishes to sink the *Blue Nymph* and all of us aboard, he will do so and there is nothing we can do to prevent it. However, I know, if we do not take our patron along, there will be no mission and no treasure. So, ask yourself, which do you trust more? Your superstitions or Allah?"

Omar and the others stared among themselves and then looked at Sinbad. He knew from their expressions while they weren't happy with the situation, they knew better than to push their captain more than they already had.

Sinbad nodded at them, then lifted the cup in front of him high into the air.

"THIS WILL BE NO PLACE FOR A WOMAN."

"So, my friends, let us enjoy tonight. For if the sun rises tomorrow, we will set out on the greatest adventure of our lives."

The next week flew by as the crew finished their preparations for the mysterious trip. They were careful to get supplies from many sources to try to hide the nature of the mission and laid on more victuals and water than they actually were going to need to give the impression they were off for a long trip.

The evening before the *Blue Nymph* sat sail, Sinbad and Omar stood at the rail, watching the sky turn from red to a dull purple as the stars began appearing in the east. They watched as a group of merchants were admitted to the deck of the ship. After some brisk trading, all but one departed. If he hadn't been watching, Sinbad wouldn't have noticed Tishimi spiriting Adara and her gear away before anyone had the chance to realize she was there.

"I'm telling you, Captain. I have a bad feeling about this. There's too much secrecy involved, and I've gotten reports that some of our crew noticed the same people watching the ship by day the closer we've gotten to sailing. I suspect we'll encounter some trouble long before we reach port."

"Let them try, Omar. The *Blue Nymph* can outrun any dhow or xebec on the seven seas and even if they get the headwinds, we can still outfight any crew out there. No, it would be a truly desperate group that tried to intercept us."

"Aye, and that's what worries me. If they do try something, they're either desperate or overly confident. Either way, it would make for quite the fight. And Allah take me, he would set the desperate against us, just to test our resolve."

"Well, in that case, make sure the ship and the armory is ready, Omar. You're the first mate. If you believe there's going to be trouble, then who am I to doubt you? Make whatever preparations you believe are prudent."

"Then, begging the Captain's pardon for my presumption, but I recommend we set sail as soon as the moon sets tonight instead of waiting for morning. We do ourselves no favors by letting any possible enemies get the jump on us."

"Now you're thinking like a first mate. I agree wholeheartedly. Spread the word among the crew. Have them bed down and dim the lights as if we were settling in for the night but put Haroun aloft to spy the docks and double the guard. We'll slip our ropes and drift a bit before setting our sails for Muscat."

Omar gave him a knowing nod in agreement before letting out a laugh. "If we return from this trip, Captain, it'll be a story that no one will believe. At least not until they see our bounty."

"Don't go spending gems you don't have yet. Omar. I suspect Allah will want to see us earn this treasure, not just plop it into our laps."

"Even so, a hard-won treasure is the best kind to spend. Besides, there was this young woman I met in town. Perhaps I will consider settling down again."

Sinbad could only look up at the heavens and mutter a quick prayer over his love-foolish first mate before retiring below. He made his way to Tishimi's cabin and knocked. After a short wait, the door inched open and Tishimi verified he was alone before opening the door just wide enough for Sinbad to enter. Adara's gear was carefully stored in one corner, and she was sitting on the edge of the spare bed, still dressed in the oversized caftan and robes that hid her sex from anyone watching the ship. Her head was uncovered though, and her red hair cascaded down over her shoulders and back.

"How is everything going?" she asked, as Sinbad closed the door behind him.

"We're going to set sail tonight as soon as the moon sets. You don't have anything else coming to the ship, do you?"

"No, I knew you were ready to sail and anything I couldn't bring with me, I will secure once we reach Muscat. We are running against a deadline, so I am travelling as lightly as possible."

"Until we are nearly at Muscat, I'm going to ask that you remain in this room during daylight hours. While we do not anticipate trouble, there are signs the ship is under observation. It is possible if there is an unknown enemy out there, they may have people assigned to watch for us from passing boats or the shore. It would be best if they could not confirm any suspicions that you are on this boat."

"As you will, Sinbad. I understood once I came aboard that there could only be one person in charge. Whatever you believe is best, I will certainly comply."

"Good. I'm willing to accept suggestions from anyone, but on the *Blue Nymph,* my word is law. Only Allah can overrule my decisions."

Adara nodded in consent. "Besides, the night on this trip will be useful to work more with the lodestone and sextant. Once we enter the Rub al-Khali, there can be no mistakes, or we'll die of thirst if the div don't take us first."

Now, that's a cheery thought. "Let us hope it doesn't come to that. Almost everyone on my crew is competent with navigation, but if there are some tricks to your items, please ensure others can use them should something happen. Allah protects those who have taken precautions before there is trouble. To wait until there is a crisis is to tempt divine retribution."

Adara began storing her gear for the upcoming trip. "If we're sailing soon, I'll need to get things ready. If you don't mind, Captain, there are some things not to be shown to just any man, even if he is the captain of the ship."

He stared at her for a second, then the tips of his ears began to get hot as he realized what she was saying. "Ah yes. If you will excuse me."

Tishimi's soft laughter followed him out of the cabin, and he hurried back to the deck of the ship as if a djinn pursued him.

Two days out of Basrah, the *Blue Nymph* was dancing on the waves as the ship made its way south by southeast down the Gulf bound for the shores of Oman. The dawn was late coming and the fog was sweeping across the gulf from the Arabian shore. Omar was frowning at his position at the helm, muttering vile things barely under his breath.

"What troubles you, Omar? We've sailed through worse fog and emerged unscathed."

"True, Captain, but this is not the season for fog to be this thick. I swear, Allah must think I have the hide of an elephant to keep throwing these thorns at me. Just once, I'd love to make a transit past Bahrain without something going wrong."

Sinbad slapped his first mate on the shoulder as he walked past. "If Allah truly sent as many tests at you as you claim, you'd be up for sainthood by now. It's just fog, Omar. Let us take in some sail and move ahead. How far from the shore are we?"

"We should be more than a mile out, so I'm not worried about shoals or reefs. Still, something is bothering me. Something unnatural moves within that fog."

Henri walked up to Sinbad, a worried look on his face. "I'm inclined to agree with Omar, Captain. There's something not right about that fog. Look closely. The edges do not seem to disperse as the air warms. This doesn't seem like any fog I've ever seen in this region."

Sinbad laughed but decided to take a closer look for himself. Picking up his spyglass, he noted the fog was thickening, instead of dispersing as the sun rose in the sky. It almost seemed as if the fog was reaching out for the *Blue Nymph*.

"Perhaps I laughed a little too quickly. Ralf, come take the wheel. Omar, have the men reef the sails. Haroun, keep a close eye for any movement within that fog bank."

The crew of the *Blue Nymph* moved as one to prepare the ship for whatever was coming their way. Seamen rushed up the ropes to take in the sails while Henri moved to a point on the bow of the ship, his arrows already nocked. Tishimi appeared at Sinbad's side as silent as a shadow, her hands resting easily on the hilts of her blades.

"Our passenger?"

"Two men guard her door. I thought I would be more useful here."

Sinbad nodded. If Tishimi felt she was needed, her fighting skills more than made up for the two crewmen below. Just as the crew finished securing the ship, the *Blue Nymph* slid into the fog bank. The little bit of sail left hanging drooped immediately as the cool morning breeze disappeared. The ship moved forward on momentum alone, and all the sailors moved to the weapons locker to prepare for whatever lurked in this thrice-damned gloom.

Just as the waiting had almost become unbearable, the ship shuddered and ground to a halt, sending the crew and any loose cargo tumbling toward the bow. There was a yelp from above, and Sinbad looked up to see Haroun hanging by one hand from a rope out over the waves.

Before he could speak, Omar piped up. "Monkey! Quit goofing around up there and get back to your post."

"I am fine, may Allah grace you for your concern."

"I'm going to grace you with the flat of my blade if you don't get back up there."

Haroun pulled himself back into the rope webbing and climbed back up to his position in the tops of the masts, as Sinbad rushed over to his first mate. "Omar, I thought you said there were no reefs out here."

"There aren't according to the charts."

Henri looked over the edge of the ship. "Captain, it's impossible, but we're snarled in a net."

"A net? Out here?"

"Ship approaching off the starboard, Captain. Making straight for us," cried Haroun from his position aloft. A few seconds later, he called again, "Another ship approaching from port."

"You were right, Omar, this was no natural fog. They've snared us like a fat rabbit." He moved to midship and then raised his voice. "Well, boys, get yourself ready. We'll teach these pirates that *this* rabbit has teeth! Take your place along the rail and among the cargo. Stay low. Don't let them know where you are until I signal."

Sinbad motioned for Ralf to leave the rudder and go below. The giant man moved down the line and tapped several men to follow him. With the trap set as well as he could make it. Sinbad could only pray they were intent on boarding the ship, not ramming and sinking his pride.

After a few anxious minutes, he heard something moving in the water and knew the two ships were moving up next to him. He took a deep breath and waited for the thud of a plank being dropped onto his deck before he stood up and with a great shout met the first of the boarders while they were still on the planks. There was a sudden motion and a scream as the first two men were shoved off the plank into the grinding water between the two ships. After that, it quickly became a free-for-all. There were too many to keep them from making the deck of the *Blue Nymph*, but Sinbad's sailors made the unknown enemy pay for every inch of deck they took.

Sinbad found himself facing three pirates. He seized a scimitar from a fallen pirate and used the two blades he now wielded as both weapon and shield. With a sudden kick, he pushed one of the pirates back and was able to slip his blade beneath the guard of another, running about a foot of good Damascus steel into the pirate's belly. Sinbad wheeled to avoid the overhead smash from the third and dodged his way back to the raised stern of the ship.

A quick glance showed Tishimi weaving her swords with unearthly precision, each cut leaving a pirate writhing on the deck. Haroun was firing arrows down onto the ship to the left while Henri was engaging archers on the other ship. William Byrne and Omar were fighting back-to-back, easily thrashing those foolish enough to come within range of their weapons.

The pirates' leaders were trying to rally their men when with a roar, Ralf charged out of the hold, a huge box of cargo held over his head. He launched his improvised missile into the midst of the pirates, bowling many over. As the rest of his team swarmed out of the hold, Ralf picked up his huge, double-headed battle axe and waded into the horde. This second wave of attackers broke the pirates' nerve, and they began fleeing back to their ships. Sinbad and the crew pressed them and caught many on the gangplanks, but the pirates quickly dumped the planks, sending some of their own men into the waters between the ships, crushing them between tons of wood.

Sinbad ordered his men to take shelter behind the rails as the pirate ships began to move away, their archers raining a storm of arrows onto the decks of the *Blue Nymph*. Haroun and Henri returned fire as best as they could, but soon, the fog swallowed up their attackers and the only sign there had been a fight was the bodies covering the deck and floating face down in the water below.

Sinbad moved quickly around his ship, identifying any who needed aid. Once he was certain his crew was still intact, bumps, bruises, scrapes, and wounds notwithstanding, he moved below to find his two guards were unscathed. He stuck his head inside the room to find Adara had armed herself with a slim sword and dagger, but there had been no cause to use them. Apparently, the attackers either didn't know Adara was on-board or they simply hadn't had time to try and force entrance.

"Sinbad, the fog's lifting," Omar's voice called from above deck.

He motioned to the guards to remain alert and then rushed up to the deck. The fog was visibly thinning, and the sun's rays were starting to cut through, sending little beams of illumination everywhere.

"By Allah, how can this be?"

Sinbad spun around to see one of his crewmen pointing to one of the dead pirates. As the sunlight hit it, the body slowly began to dissolve into fog, rising into the sky like steam from a pot. By the time the fog completely disappeared, so had all the pirates.

"Black magic if I've ever seen it," Henri said, staring off into the distance as if still seeking the ships that had attacked earlier.

Sinbad heard the murmurs going through his crew and stepped into the middle of them, speaking in a cheerful voice, "It appears someone does not want us to continue to Muscat. It is not the first time demons and men have conspired against the crew of the *Blue Nymph*, and it will not be the last. I swear to you men, on the nymph that graces our bow, we will continue to look danger in the eye, laugh, and show them the strength of our loyalty and our swords."

There was a momentary pause and then a lusty cheer went up among the seamen. Rafi appeared among them, directing some of them below for medical treatment, while the others swarmed over the side of the ship and began detangling the net holding the *Blue Nymph* fast.

Omar moved over next to Sinbad and spoke in a soft voice. "That was closer than I like to think. If that fog had been a little more realistic, we might have blundered straight into their trap at full speed and lost our masts."

"Aye, but all they've managed to do is let us know that someone out there is trying to stop us. I doubt they'll try anything at sea again, but let's double the watch at night just to be sure."

"I told you taking a woman aboard was bad luck."

"And I told you that without her being here, we wouldn't be on the road to a fabulous treasure."

"Or our graves."

Sinbad slapped him on the shoulder again. "Omar, I could had you a ruby the size of an orange and you'd complain that it wasn't a diamond. Come, let's get this ship moving again. Ralf, take the helm. Omar, once that netting is cleared, get all the sail she'll hold aloft. This has cost us valuable time."

Omar's sour expression moderated, and the vaguest hint of a smile crept to the corners of his mouth. "Aye, if they think something like that will stop the *Blue Nymph*, they don't know us very well."

"That's the spirit. I'm going below for a bit. Perhaps our passenger can help shed some light on this incident."

Sinbad walked through the crew, encouraging some, helping another, and had the crew moving like the team they were before slipping into the cabins below. He relieved the guards and sent them up to help with the repairs. He was unsurprised to find Tishimi already in the room, preparing her calligraphy pens and inks.

"Everything going well here?"

Tishimi bowed slightly. "The sun has risen. I thought it would be a shame to waste the opportunity."

"As you wish."

He waited for the female samurai to depart before turning to Adara. "It seems your trip is not quite as private as we had hoped."

"Oh?"

"Those were no ordinary pirates, nor were those ordinary ships. There wasn't a breath of wind, but those ships sailed away from us as if they were fueled by a hurricane. The pirate bodies turned into wisps of fog once the sun appeared. Do you have any idea who else might be after this treasure?"

"While the city of Umar is not a well-known legend, not well known does not mean unknown. Someone with skill and knowledge of sorcery could be seeking the same treasures we are. Some of the rumored items would be of great interest to a wizard. After all, it's said that Umar was buried by Allah for creating beings and magical items which were anathema to him. I can think of many nations who might dream of finding objects like that to further their aims."

"But that's not what you're after?"

Adara crossed her legs and smiled seductively at Sinbad. "No, I do not seek to be cursed. I am a simple woman, Sinbad. I like jewels. I like gold. And…" she paused looking him up and down before continuing, "I like men. Not necessarily in that order, but what would I do with a magic scimitar or a staff that commanded djinn? I'm no warrior and dealing with the djinn is more dangerous than walking across the desert without a water bottle. No, you'll find me a rather simple businesswoman."

"Adara, there is nothing simple about you and I don't believe for a second that you don't know more about this situation than you're telling me. But I have agreed to take you to the city and to seize its treasures. I am not a man to go back on my word, but mark this. If I discover you have been untruthful to me, if you endanger my crew or my ship, then you'll find me a most implacable enemy."

"Sinbad, Sinbad, do *I* look like I want to make enemies? I want this trip to go as smoothly as possible. As I said, there may be others who seek the city. After all, if I could find the information, others could find it too. But, since they do not have my map, or my lodestone, so if it's a race, then it's a race we should win and win easily."

"I'll believe it'll be easy when we're sailing back to Basrah with the treasures. Always assume something can go wrong. That's how I've stayed alive this long."

"Not to hear Henri speaking."

"Henri is a born pessimist."

By the end of the week, the *Blue Nymph* was tied to the docks of Muscat and Sinbad had made the arrangements for a caravan. It had taken some time to decide who was going to go into the desert and who was going to remain behind, but for every man they took into the desert, it meant that much more weight in food and water. It was important not to make their caravan look too ostentatious, to avoid thieves and bandits tracking them out of the city, but then again, they couldn't make their caravan so small it invited the same fate.

Omar came by later in the day, covered with dust and bearing the same expression as the camels he had been wrangling. "By Allah's voice, Sinbad, preparing a ship for a voyage to unknown seas takes less preparation than this journey. If we need to make all speed, we need to get this caravan moving sooner than later. There's only so much camel smell I can take."

"Better get used to it now, friend, because once we start, that's about all your going to be smelling for the next few weeks."

"Bah!"

Omar stomped off in a huff, but Sinbad knew as long as Omar was complaining, everything was going well. He rolled up the paper containing the list of supplies left to be procured when there was a strange shadow at the door.

A small, wizened man stood there, dressed better than the average merchant. He had the air of belonging to a noble's retinue, but not a noble himself. "Pardon me, *effendi*, do you know where I could find the esteemed Sinbad, the captain of the famous *Blue Nymph,* that has so recently appeared in our harbor?"

"You are in good luck, my fine fellow, for I am Sinbad."

"Allah be praised. I am Ishmi, a messenger for the Emir. He has requested your presence at a dinner party this evening. You may bring as many of your crew as you wish."

"A dinner party you say?"

"Yes, *sahib*, it will start one hour after dark, this evening. He has promised to make it quite worth your while if you can spare a few minutes to have a private conversation with him."

"You may tell the Emir that my crew and I would be honored to attend. Will you be our guide to his residence?"

"It shall be as you wish. I shall seek you out at sundown."

"I look forward to this. Thank you, Ishmi," Sinbad said, tossing a sack of coins to the wizened man. "Those are for you. If you need them not, distribute them to the poor and widows you encounter on your way back."

"Allah thank your generosity."

As soon as the small man left, Henri appeared from a back room. "Do you think this is on the up and up?"

"Who is to say? However, if you'd like to see where he's going?"

"Consider it done."

The Gaul pulled on a hooded robe and belted it closed around his waist. He glanced out to the door to see which way the small man had gone and then slipped out and was quickly lost to sight in the milling crowd.

Sinbad sent some runners out and shortly the rest of his crew had joined him in the small building he had rented for his stay in Muscat. He explained the situation to them and asked their opinions.

Ralf spoke up first. "I don't like it, Sinbad. It smells of a trap, after what happened out on the sea. Invited the entire crew? Seems like a great opportunity to gather up the sheep for slaughter."

Rafi stroked his long white beard before replying. "While the histories are long about rulers who have their own motives for doing what they do, I also do not see that we gain anything by refusing to attend. After all, we are strangers in his lands and to throw his hospitality back in his face would be the height of rudeness. One could say, we'd be giving him the reason he might be looking for by not attending."

"I would tend to agree with Rafi," Byrne said, nodding in the doctor's direction. "I know from my own experience that antagonizing a more powerful clan leader should only be done if you know you've got the strength to meet him head on or a great escape plan. Now, that doesn't mean we should go in unsuspecting-like. Henri may be rubbing off on me, but a little caution from time to time is not a bad thing.

"William has hit the nail on the head," Omar said, his burly arms crossed over his chest. "We gain nothing by refusing to go and potentially alienate a possible ally. Then again, Sinbad didn't say how many of the crew were going to attend. I would recommend a small group attend, with another group lurking nearby to provide aid should it turn out to be a trap."

Sinbad smiled at his first mate. "A most reasonable suggestion, Omar. Well, good friends, we have much to do to get our caravan ready today. Afterwards, we need to certainly get fresh baths and new clothes for us all." He waved a hand in front of his nose before winking at Omar. "Especially our first mate.

"WE GAIN NOTHING BY REFUSING TO GO."

It would not do to introduce a two-legged camel to his eminence, would it?"

Omar retreated from the group, muttering dire threats against all assembled there, and Sinbad waved the rest out to finish their assignments. Adara waited until everyone else had left before speaking with Sinbad.

"And what of me? I do not believe it would do us any good to announce my presence here."

"My lady, I have no doubt your presence is exactly why we've been invited to this soiree. How our enemies got to Muscat ahead of us is beyond my understanding. However, if they *are* here, it stands to reason they have either suborned the Emir to their cause or at least roused his curiosity. If he is merely curious, then we can possibly swing him to our side. If he is an enemy, better to find out here than in the middle of the desert surrounded by his troops."

"You're playing a dangerous game, Sinbad. There's every chance we'll go into that palace and never leave."

"And there's always the chance we'll not only leave, but with full bellies and full pockets. I can see you've been hanging around Omar too long. Life sends enough troubles to weigh us down as it is. Do not go looking to add more to your shoulders. There's no point in worrying about that which you have no control over. I have faith in my crew and myself that we'll slip through any snare set in our path."

"I wish I had your confidence."

"Sail with us more often and you just might."

"An interesting offer, Sinbad, but that's a conversation for another day. We are still against a deadline. We must leave no later than tomorrow evening if we are to get to our destination on time."

"If Allah wills, it will happen.

"Indeed. If Allah wills. . . ."

The rest of the day went smoothly and as he had said, Ishmi appeared at the door of Sinbad's house just as the sun was setting behind the buildings of Muscat. Sharp, dark shadows seemed to envelop the streets, and a hot, dry wind blew in off the desert, making even the thinnest of clothing feel like they were thick furs.

"Ah, *effendi* Sinbad. I am here as promised."

"Allah bless you for being a man of your word, Ishmi. Please give me a moment to gather my friends and we will leave shortly."

Sinbad stepped through a connecting door and motioned for his party to follow him. A second group, led by Henri and William would set out a few minutes after Sinbad had left, taking a route Henri had reconnoitered, giving them a clear view over the wall into the palace's grounds.

Ishmi's eyes settled on the two women who were accompanying the group.

Tishimi had agreed to wear one of her few remaining formal kimonos to the function, but she had refused to go without her weapons strapped to her waist. Sinbad knew better than to ask her to leave them behind, but the black lacquered sheaths stood out in sharp contrast to the light blue kimono with the white Sakura pattern.

Adara was dressed in black silks that set off her red hair and she had put a scarf over her head and face, so only her eyes were visible.

Ishmi took several deep breaths before speaking. "*Effendi*, I was not informed that you had female companions. I would have arranged a carriage for them had I known. I apologize for the inconvenience."

Adara let out a small laugh. "It is most forgiven. That you show such concern is apology enough."

"As you wish. The Emir awaits, so if you would please come with me."

Thanks to Henri's report, Sinbad knew the emir's palace wasn't far away and after a bit, the party arrived at the front gates. The guards spoke to Ishmi, and then came over to speak to Sinbad.

"I am sorry to inconvenience you, but we must ask that any and all weapons must be left with us before you may enter."

"A most unusual request."

The guard looked embarrassed, but he continued. "Be that as it may, it is our orders from the Emir and though the name of Sinbad is known far and wide among the lands, it is not worth my life to go against an order of my emir."

"Can one of you take a request to the emir for me?"

"It can be done."

"Ask the emir if we surrender our weapons, that our companion there," he motioned to Tishimi, "be allowed to keep hers. She is a foreigner to our shores and her customs are different. Besides, surely the emir would not fear the blades of a young woman?"

"*Effendi*, you've sailed the world and know the blade of a young woman can be the most dangerous of all, but I will send someone to convey your request to the emir."

The party divested itself of their weapons and it was quite an eclectic collection of weapons that rested on a table just within the palace walls. Scimitars, long swords, bows, and daggers of all shapes and sizes were aligned neatly and the guards noted that even the humblest weapon was well maintained and quite deadly.

Shortly after Henry divested the last dagger he had hidden on his body, the messenger reappeared and whispered to the head guard. The tall Mameluke nodded and then spoke to Sinbad. "His eminence has agreed to your request. He also puts you personally in charge of your companion and any problems they may cause will fall on you twice as hard."

"A perfectly acceptable bargain. Now, I believe the emir is waiting for us."

The Mameluke waved a huge hand, and two courtiers appeared and led the party within the palace grounds. They moved through the halls of the palace until they reached a center courtyard where a banquet had been laid out. The courtyard was filled with people dressed in their finery and waiters moved among them carrying trays of food and wine.

There was the sound of a gong and the crowd grew quiet as all eyes fell on the party entering the courtyard. Someone off to the side spoke loud enough for all to hear. "Excellency, Captain Sinbad of the *Blue Nymph* and party."

A large, portly man came off the center dais and made his way toward Sinbad. "Ah, good day. Good day, Captain. I am so glad you accepted my invitation to this little banquet. Come, come, I've heard so much about you and your fabulous trips, you must tell me about them over some food."

Sinbad found himself caught up in the whirlwind of the emir's excitement and before he knew exactly what had happened, he found himself seated on a large, pillowed chair with the emir and several others sitting around him asking him questions about his earlier voyages and so on. Glancing up, he saw his crew was suffering a similar fate as different people were gathering around them, asking questions and taking in their answers. Tishimi was doing her best to be polite, but Sinbad knew he was going to hear about this after they returned. On her best day she was not fond of crowds, but to be in a maelstrom of people like this was likely to strain her legendary patience.

He turned his attention back to the Emir, who was watching him with much curiosity. "So, tell me, Sinbad, what brings such a famous sailor as you to Muscat? I hear you are hiring a caravan, but to the east, north, and west of here is naught but desert. Surely there's nothing there of interest to such an august personality as yourself?"

"Ah, I am sorry to disappoint, your eminence, but even the boldest of adventurers must occasionally take a simple commission to earn a living. Ships do not maintain themselves. We are merely here to take a load of cargo into the interior. The tribe of Ali bin Suliman is travelling along the coast, driving their herds toward Yemen and we were commissioned to deliver some goods to them and in return, we are to receive some spices the tribe was able to secure from Ethiopia. Merely a trifling matter for one as esteemed as yourself."

"Is that so? I dare not claim to know every tribe, but I am unfamiliar with the tribe of Ali Bin Suliman."

"I honestly would be surprised if you had met them, oh wisest of rulers. They are a small tribe, but their leader once rescued me when I had a mishap before I acquired my current ship. They occasionally contact me when there are things they cannot acquire for themselves. It is mere happenstance they are within a few weeks ride from Muscat as they tend to stay mostly in the western part of this desert."

The look the emir gave Sinbad told him he didn't believe a word Sinbad was saying, but he couldn't prove otherwise . . . yet. They continued making small talk and the emir offered to show Sinbad around the city, but Sinbad begged off, stating his crew must finish their preparations, lest they miss the tribe in the delay.

After several hours of dining and mingling, Sinbad gave his crew the high sign and carefully, one after the other extricated themselves from their throngs of admirers and made their way to the palace gates. Once he saw the last had left, he approached the emir to say his goodbyes.

"Your eminence, your generosity and your larder are second only to Allah himself. I have not been feted so well in all my life, but if you can grant me your grace, I believe I should take my leave."

"Ah, Sinbad, it has been such a short visit. I had hoped to convince you to stay in Muscat a few more days, but then again, as you said, you have promised to meet your customers, and it would be highly selfish of me to cause you to break your word on my behalf."

"You are too kind. When I return to Muscat, I would love to take you up on your invitation."

"If it is the will of Allah, I look forward to that day."

Eventually, Sinbad managed to gracefully slip away from the Emir and after retrieving his weapons from the Mameluke, began walking back to his rented house. He had not gone far before he heard a whisper from an alleyway and he moved quickly to join Henri who was waiting in the shadows.

"I think a round-about way would be the safest way to reach our abode."

Sinbad immediately began scanning the nearby shadows. "Has something happened?"

"That depends on your definition of something. William reports that as soon as we left for the party, a group of men dressed in black descended on our house. While nothing appears to be out of place, it was thoroughly searched. Also, Tishimi and Omar report being attacked by a group of thieves after they'd gone but a few blocks from the palace. Needless to say, the attackers were quickly scattered. Omar reports they all appeared too well-armed and too well-fed to be common thieves."

"It is as I suspected. This party was a mere ruse to try and elicit information from us and injure or delay us before we can leave the city."

Henri glanced around, nocking and unnocking the arrow in his hand in his nervousness. "I do not like this, Sinbad. This mission has an evil feel to it.

Are you certain you wish to continue?"

"Henri, I want to continue more than ever. The enemy has shown its hand, even if we aren't certain what their ultimate goal is. Here is what I want you to do. At first light, go to the docks and have the crew manning the *Blue Nymph* take it out to sea after the moon sets tomorrow night. Sail about fifty miles down the coast. There, they should find a small harbor. It's not much, but it's sheltered from the winds and sea. Remain there for three weeks. If we have not appeared, sail to Aden for supplies and then return along the coast. If we have missed them, we'll start moving west along the coast to meet them. I do not want the *Blue Nymph* to remain somewhere the emir can keep it under observation. Perhaps I'm overthinking this, but if we find the treasures we believe are awaiting us, it would be best not to tempt the emir's curiosity a second time."

"It shall be done, Sinbad."

The trip back to the rented house was made in silence as the two men flitted from shadow to shadow as quietly as cats on a thick carpet. After a roundabout trek through the streets and alleys of Muscat, they were approaching their destination when two large shadows detached from the depths of a nearby alley and moved to intercept. Sinbad drew his scimitar but was nearly taken by surprise as his opponent spread two large bat-like wings and leapt into the sky before attacking him.

The two men turned back-to-back to face their flying opponents, Henri cursed himself and the fates themselves for letting the opponents get so close he couldn't use his bow, but he soon showed he was as capable with his sword as he was his bow. The creatures flitted from the dim light into the deeper shadows, only to return at different heights and angles, forcing Sinbad and Henri into fighting defensively. They walked sideways until they were in the small square near the house, giving themselves more room to fight.

One of the shadows let out a shriek, and it was all Sinbad could do to keep his hold on his scimitar. The frequency of the shriek vibrated his whole body, but Sinbad resisted its siren call to turn and run. With a herculean effort, Sinbad brought his scimitar up in a curved strike, catching his opponent in its leg. The creature screamed in pain and flew up into the sky.

"Henri, give me your sword."

"What!?"

"Give me your sword and grab your bow. I'll try to drive them upward, where you'll have a chance to take them on the wing. Think of it as me flushing a game bird for you."

"That's just crazy enough to work."

Henri took a wild swing at his opponent, and as it swept past, he slid his sword into Sinbad's left hand before crouching down. Sinbad took a wider stance, holding each blade at the ready in both directions. When one of the creatures swooped in again, Sinbad was able to block its attack with Henri's blade and then score a hit on its shoulder with his scimitar. The creature crashed to the ground, but before Sinbad could finish it off, the other swooped in, forcing Sinbad to defend against it.

"I'm ready, Captain."

Sinbad fought back against the second opponent's onslaught, but it was forced to fly up and back to avoid Sinbad's flurry of swings. As soon as it was several feet away, Henri quickly stood up and fired point-blank into its chest. The creature screamed before falling from the sky. Sinbad turned to face the first wounded opponent as Henri took aim and sent a shaft deep into the second's head.

The first opponent spread its wings to try and take flight, but Sinbad's wound wouldn't let it do more than flutter a few feet off the ground. Sinbad rushed it and it only had time to lift its sword in a feeble parry before Sinbad drove his scimitar deep into its chest. The bale light in the creature's eyes flared and then went dim as the creature went limp and collapsed onto Sinbad. Sinbad was caught by surprise at how light the creature was, considering how powerful its blows had been, and he let the tip of his scimitar drop. The creature slid backwards off his blade to collapse onto the ground at his feet.

Henri and he shared a look of relief but when they turned to examine the creatures they had been fighting, there was a flash of light, reducing the two beings to smoldering piles of ash which slowly began wafting away in the evening breeze.

"Foul sorcery," Henri said in a hushed voice.

"Indeed. We should hurry to the house to ensure everyone else is all right."

As they approached the house, they saw lights on within. Entering, they encountered the rest of his crew except for Tishimi. Sinbad shut the windows and door before turning to face the crew. "Is everyone all right?"

Omar sat up straight in his chair with a worried look at his captain's actions. "I think the question should be, are you all right, Captain?"

"Didn't you hear Henri and I fighting for our lives not more than thirty feet from here?"

William bolted out of his chair. "That's impossible. We had the doors and windows open. If there was a fight that close, there's no way we couldn't have heard it."

Adara appeared from an adjoining room, a worried look on her face. "No, my fine Scadian, not impossible. Not if magic was involved. It's a fairly minor spell to create an area where sounds are silenced or at least muffled."

Sinbad and Henri related the tale of their fight and described their attackers as best they could. The others could only offer conjecture about the creatures. Once they started comparing stories, each realized they'd all been accosted in differing manners. Almost as if they were being tested and evaluated.

"Our shadowy opponent grows bolder," Sinbad said, taking a seat at the table. "Adara, are you certain you don't have anything to add to this conversation?"

"I certainly had not spoken to anyone else about this mission other than you. Is it possible someone divined my intentions during my own pursuit of this information? Absolutely. The information I acquired was not gathered from one place or one source. It would have been very difficult for someone to know exactly what I was seeking, but, if one was wise enough, or wealthy enough, . . ." She left the rest of her sentence hanging.

"So, our opponent may know exactly what we seek or simply know you're seeking something important . . . something important enough to send you through all that effort. Either way, we have to assume we're in a race against both time and an unknown enemy. One who is either a skilled sorcerer or has the wealth to employ one."

Sinbad leaned back in the chair and let out an honest yawn. "Very well. I have already made arrangements for the *Blue Nymph* to set sail tomorrow evening. I strongly suggest we do everything we can to quietly prepare the caravan to leave no later than midnight tomorrow night. We'll make our way out the west gate and make a show of heading along the shore. Once we are several hours from the city, we'll turn north into the desert and see just how accurate our dear benefactor's map is." He finished with a flourish in Adara's direction.

Omar made a noise and then spoke what was on many of the crew's minds. "Or we'll quickly find out how inaccurate it is."

The crew dispersed, each heading for their beds, and soon only Sinbad and Omar were sitting at the small table, a steaming cup of coffee in front of each. Both sat silently in thought until Omar broke the silence. "Do you believe the emir was behind this?"

"I honestly do not know, Omar. He knows we're here for some reason and did his best to get me to talk about it. He also knows that my story of delivering goods to a Bedouin tribe was malarky, but he was polite enough not to make an issue of it. But do I believe he is behind the attacks on us?" Sinbad paused, deep in thought. He sat motionless for a few moments before stirring himself to take a sip of the strong, thick coffee. "No. No, I don't believe so. I think he thinks we're after treasure and would like to cut himself in on some of the profits, but magical creatures swooping in from the sky? Pirates that vanish into smoke when they are killed? I just don't see it."

"But you do not trust him either?'

"No. While he wouldn't interfere with us directly, I do believe he will follow us into the desert to see where we are going. We'll have to be extra careful once we leave the city. Which is why I must ask something of you, old friend, that I hate to do."

"Oh?"

"I'm sending the *Blue Nymph* ahead to an anchorage down the coast. I want you to take charge of the ship in my absence."

Omar looked like a thundercloud had formed around his head as he leaned heavily on the table and leaned in Sinbad's direction. "You're going to need me when you get to the city, and I should be by your side."

"You are right, and we have stared the fates in the eye shoulder to shoulder in the past and we will again in the future. But the *Blue Nymph* is our lifeline. It must be well-stocked and ready to sail at a moment's notice should something go wrong. There's no one else in the world I'd trust with the ship more than you, Omar. I could command you as the captain, but I'd rather ask you as a friend to see to the ship, get her out of Muscat safely, and be standing by when we return."

Omar started to say something, but Sinbad stared deeply into his eyes, and he saw Omar's determination waiver and finally, the bulldog of a man he called friend slumped in on himself in acquiescence. "All right, Sinbad. I think you're making a mistake, but if it means that much to you. I'll take care of the *Blue Nymph* as if it were my own. Sampson isn't going to know what to do if you're not aboard though when we sail. I suspect that cat will drive me even more mad before you or Tishimi return."

"Face it, Omar, you're a cat person."

"Say that again, Captain, and you'll be walking back to Basrah."

The caravan arduously made its way up a hill, following a serpentine path past shifting sand dunes and rocky outcroppings. Sinbad swayed with the rhythm of his camel, sitting outside the tented platform centered on the beast's back. The wind had died down and he absentmindedly brushed off the sand piled against the felt tent. He found himself almost drowsing between the residual heat of the day and the undulations of the camel's back.

Another camel came up next to his, and Adara shifted her wrappings, exposing her face. "This should be the right place. We'll have to make camp on the summit of this hill."

"I hope your map is true. It's three days ride back to the last oasis. Of course, calling that mudhole an oasis was giving it too much honor. Even the camels seemed upset they had to drink that water."

Adara favored him with a smile, recognizing Sinbad's grousing as his way of passing the time. "Better muddy water than no water, but no, unless something is horribly wrong, our destination awaits at the end of this trail."

Sinbad shifted his shoulders, trying to work a kink out of them. "When will we reach the city?"

"Tomorrow night. The moon shall be at its fullest then. Only then will the city be revealed to those fated to reach it."

"Very poetic, but not very helpful."

"You'll understand when you see it, Sinbad. Once the city is revealed, it will only remain for the three nights the moon is the fullest. If we have not left the city by that time, we will be trapped there."

"So you've said. Then let us get to the top and make our preparations."

Adara nodded in agreement and then let her camel slow down to fall back into its place in the line. From the tent behind him, Haroun stuck his head out, "Do you need relief, Captain? There's not much to do back here but sit and try to keep my stomach in place."

"Haroun, you scamper among the rigging like you were born to it and I've seen you maintain your position in the roughest of seas. Now you tell me that riding a camel makes you seasick?"

"It's not the riding per se but riding in this damnable tent. I know we needed to use them against the sandstorms, but at sea, I can keep my eyes on the horizon. I would have the same issues I'm having now if you made me sail the entire voyage working in the cargo hold. No, if I can see where we are going and what is happening, I have no problems, but as a blind passenger? My mind and my stomach are of two differing opinions."

"Well, then by all means, Haroun, at least open the flaps and sit at the edge of the tent. We are almost at our destination and the air is quiet. I do not believe we will need to take shelter before we dismount for the night."

"Praise be, Captain." Haroun threw the tent flaps back and secured them before sitting cross-legged in the entrance of the tent. "Have you given thought to what's going to happen at the end of this journey?"

Sinbad stared up the hill they were climbing trying to estimate how much further they had to go. "No, Haroun, nothing definitive. I have played out many scenarios in my mind, but until we see the lay of the land, there's no point in setting my mind to one scheme or another. No, we're going to have to be flexible depending on what Allah has in store for us."

"To be honest, Captain, I'll be glad when this is over. There's been entirely too much sorcery and not enough treasure to whet my whistle."

"... AT LEAST OPEN THE FLAPS AND SIT AT THE EDGE ..."

"Now, that's the Haroun I'm used to dealing with. What would you do with a king's ransom worth of treasures?"

Haroun's eyes lit up. "What else, Captain? I'd buy my own ship and join your fleet. Why the pirates from Spain to Cathay would flee the seas knowing Captain Sinbad had many ships under his command. Course, that might get a little boring if is no one to challenge us, but such is the price of success."

Sinbad laughed, caught up in his crewman's exuberance. "Well, then, if you're Captain Haroun, who would I be?"

"Why you would have to be an Admiral if you had your own fleet, unless you prefer to be the Emir of the Sea? We could find an island and establish our own kingdom on it. Fighting ships and merchants would flock to your island and perhaps even the Caliph of Baghdad might have to come calling."

"Woah ho, Haroun? An emir? Me? No, my good friend, I am not one who'd be comfortable lounging around in a sterile, gray palace, waited on hand and foot. I'm quite content simply leading the *Blue Nymph*, enjoying the company of good friends and a good crew. A little bounty now and then is not a bad thing either, but me? Sitting on some stuffy throne and dealing with endless meetings and supplicants wanting this or that? No, I'll be happy to set you up there."

"As you wish, Captain. However, if I were to become Emir of the Sea, I would immediately install you as my First Admiral."

"If you become Emir of the Sea, Haroun, I'd be the first to volunteer for the assignment."

The two continued bantering for a bit until Sinbad noticed the trail was leveling off. Glancing ahead, he saw they had almost reached the summit, and the camels were picking up speed, as if they too knew their destination was almost in reach.

Cresting the ridge, Sinbad saw the top of the hill was almost flat. It made him feel as if a djinn had taken a huge sword and lopped the top of the hill off, leaving this plain behind. There was a large depression in the center of the hill, and a small grove of palm trees off to one side. The camels were making their way toward the grove and Sinbad could smell the dates growing on the trees ahead.

As soon as they reached the grove, the camels knelt, allowing their riders to dismount. Sinbad sent three men ahead to search through the grove to ensure they were alone, and once they had returned with their report, he dispatched the crew to unload the camels, set up the tents, and to stake the camels out near the grove where they could reach the water. Once the camp was established, he sent men to various spots along the edge of the butte to keep a look out for any signs of approaching trouble.

The moon was just rising over the far edge of the hill when Adara sought him out. She checked her map against the readings she got from her lodestone and the sextant and then looked at him triumphantly. "We are exactly where we are supposed to be and in time too. Sinbad, we have done it."

"Not quite, Adara. There is no city."

She pointed at the huge moon, low on the horizon. "There will be. Soon, the city of Umar will be revealed, and its treasures will be ours."

Sinbad laughed, although it was impossible to miss the excitement in his eyes too. "Let's not start spending that treasure before it is within our grasp. After all, there is a reason this city disappeared all those years ago and another why the treasure may still be there. I know we have a tight window to search for and secure that treasure but rushing blindly into a haunted city is never a good idea."

She wagged a finger at him. "And this is the brave adventurer who laughs in the face of danger?"

"This is the face of a man who's seen his fair share of danger and has always managed to find his way back to his home port, because I don't fear danger. However, I also do not believe I am invulnerable. If I can get in and get out without having to fight off ravenous beasts, murderous bandits, or desert demons, then I will be the happiest adventurer in the entire Caliphate."

Their bantering was interrupted by Henri who came rushing over. "Sinbad, our lookouts report a small cloud of dust about a day's ride behind us."

"Who could it be?" Adara asked.

Sinbad thought for a moment before answering. "If I had to guess, I'd say the Emir's curiosity has led him to send men to shadow our trail. I suspect they've been behind us this entire way. Whether they mean to attack or are simply trying to see what led us off the coastal trail deep into the Rub al'-Khali, only Allah can say. Still, unless they show themselves hostile, there's not much I can do. If they approach, seeking water, I must allow them access. If they wish to camp, again, I have no reason to turn them away. After all, Allah provided the shade and the water, not I. I have no more claim on this than that camel over there."

He thought some more and then spoke to Henri. "Have the lookouts keep close watch on that cloud. It could be a patrol, or it could be a smaller group trying to raise dust to make us think they are in one spot while the main body seeks a different route to the summit. We will not take aggressive action against them unless they force our hand but have everyone remain under arms. We'll sleep in shifts tonight."

Henri saluted and rushed off to spread the word. As soon as Henri was out of hearing range, Adara spun toward Sinbad. "But, if they are allowed to reach the summit, they cannot help but see the city when it appears tomorrow night."

"It is a problem, to be sure, but what is the alternative? Pit my crewmen against unknown numbers of men when it may not be a problem at all. No, I'll not be the aggressor against those who may mean me no harm."

"Your generous heart may be your downfall yet, Sinbad."

"If so, I'll go to Paradise knowing I treated my fellow man well. I do not seek out fame and fortune at the cost of others, Adara. I may have done things I am not proud of in the past, but I'd rather be generous with whatever life sends me than a parsimonious man clinging to every coin. My friends and my companions make me already richer than any caliph or emir . . . and I don't have to sleep with guards at my bedside."

Adara waved her hand in an encompassing motion, pointing to the guards moving through the camp. "Oh?"

Sinbad laughed before bowing to her and heading toward his tent. "Well . . . not every night."

The next day was one of the longest Sinbad could remember. The sun beat down unmercifully on the hilltop and the few trees around the oasis provided only meager shade. Luckily, the waterhole was clear and the water cool, so no one suffered overmuch from thirst. Sinbad ensured runners took water out to the men posted on guard on the perimeters of the camp and brought back periodic reports.

Sinbad had gathered his crew leaders together to discuss their options should they successfully acquire the treasures of Umar. There had been no sign of any movement, so either the group spotted yesterday had taken advantage of the cool of night to keep traveling, or else they were content to wait where they were until they saw signs that Sinbad's caravan was moving on. If it was the former, then there was no problem, but if it was the latter? Sinbad's forehead wrinkled at the thought of that possibility. Were his pursuers, if that's what they were, so well-equipped they could stay away from the oasis without worry? If so, that implied they were no ordinary bandits.

"Adara, does your map show any other routes back to the coast without returning on the same route we arrived?"

"There is, Sinbad, but it would be an arduous journey at best. We would have to take at least five days more water than we usually carry to reach one of the identified oases and the sand in that region is treacherous. We could lose men and camels to the shifting sands before we knew they were in danger."

"But it could be done?"

"It could, but I wouldn't unless there was absolutely no other way. According to the legends, the djinn in that region are a jealous sort and they love to trick travelers into getting lost and leading them into dangerous situations. However, if it's that or facing certain death by steel, I might agree that the djinn are the lesser threat."

Ralf let out a boisterous laugh. "Evil men or evil spirts. One way or the other, Sinbad, this is shaping up to be an adventure to remember."

Tishimi looked up from the drawing she was working on, "There are legends of the *oni* in my country being bribed with gifts or gems to leave travelers alone. Can your Arabian demons be similarly appeased?"

"It all depends on which storyteller you ask, Tishimi. The few I've had the misfortune to encounter had to be dealt with by force. My shoulders and neck still remember the feel of the one being I was forced to carry for a week or more. No, I'm going to assume if we encounter a being like that, it'll depend on our good steel and sharp reflexes to win the day."

William Byrne lifted his drinking cup toward Sinbad. "Sounds like the legends of the fae back in my country. Some of them are more mischievous and they like their shiny things well enough that a few gems or something shiny and pretty and they're happy to leave you alone. Others though, were a bloodthirsty lot. Offering them treasure only told them what to look for once they had dismembered your body. And the trouble is, some of them looked so much alike, you didn't know which you were dealing with until it was too late."

Ralf nodded in agreement. "Aye, the fae are a tricky lot. And, quick to twist your words around to their own liking when you deal with them. Trust not a dwarf's gold or an elf's smile."

Henri banged his glass down on the table. "Well, now that we're all acquainted with the boogiemen in our respective cultures, how do we deal with the real threat. Those men just out of sight to the south? I'm much more worried about getting a foot of steel in my belly than I am in being dragged into a fairy circle and dancing until dawn when we try to leave."

Sinbad laughed. "Ah, Henri. And here I thought you were such the romantic. I have not forgotten about them, but honestly, until nightfall tonight, there is little we can do. Either the city will appear or it will not . . ."

"It *will* appear," Adara interjected, a tone of finality in her voice.

"Excuse me, when it appears, then we can investigate, seize the treasures, defeat whatever would stop us and then we'll decide on how to deal with our uninvited guests. If they're still there and if they'll wait that long."

"Still wish you had let Haroun and I reconnoiter their positions."

"Henri, they were too far away when they were last seen. There was no way for the two of you to get there and back before moonrise tonight. No, I trust you have positioned the lookouts as well as anyone could. Now, all we can do is try to stay out of the sun and wait."

Ralf looked up at the clear blue sky. "At least the breeze is fresh, Captain. I do not believe we're going to have any issues with sandstorms or worse for a few days."

Rafi glanced at Ralf, a worried look on his face. "Ralf, why must you constantly tempt fate?"

"Because fate doesn't need to be tempted. One learns to read the signs after all these years of sailing, Captain. I prefer a rough sea over a calm one. At least, when something happens on a rough sea, everyone's already prepared. A calm sea invites relaxing one's guard."

"Begging the captain's pardon, but may I make a medical opinion, Captain?"

"Of course, Rafi, you do not need my permission to do your job."

"Then I would recommend everyone who's going into the city this evening stop by my tent, enjoy some of the fresh fruit I brought along and then retire to their tents for the afternoon. Try to get as much sleep as possible. Tired crewmen make mistakes, and when entering a cursed city, it would be best to limit mistakes as much as possible."

"Rafi, I think you're just tired of listening to us argue, but your point is well taken. We'll take a small group into the city tonight. If needed, we can return the second night with a larger crew to recover whatever we find. But, since we do not know the lay of the city nor what might guard it after all these years, a small group moving quickly is probably the best way to make our first attempt. So, if you'll all follow Rafi, we'll reconvene here just after dark and wait for the moonrise."

As the full moon rose like a pearl emerging out of the dark sea, a shimmering glow began to emanate from the depression in the center of the butte. A silver aura rose from the ground and took the ghostly form of a city. Looking closely, Sinbad could see a central keep rising at the center of the city, towering over the buildings hinted at beyond the ghostly city wall. Finally, as the moon rose three hands above the horizon, the Forbidden City of Umar was revealed. Even though everything appeared solid, there was an unearthly silver aura surrounding the area, ensuring no one would presume this to be just another city.

"By Allah, I never thought I would behold such a sight," Rafi said in a soft voice. "Even if no treasures lie within, to simply see something that should not be is a treasure in and of itself."

Sinbad clapped his friend on the shoulder. "While I understand your sentiment, Rafi, if there is no treasure, this has been a very expensive sightseeing trip. Come, my friends, it's time to see what Umar holds."

The small group of people left the shelter of the trees toward the newly revealed city. The gates stood open and to Sinbad's relief, no ghostly sentries stood on the walls. Once within the city, they couldn't help but notice how ordinary it appeared. If not for the ghostly aura, it would have looked perfectly at home next to Baghdad or Muscat.

Sinbad motioned everyone closer. "The city seems deserted, but appearances can be deceiving. We'll break into teams of two and move toward the citadel. If there is any treasure worth finding, that is the logical place. However, if we each approach from a different angle, we'll be certain not to miss anything."

The crew nodded assent and ensured their weapons were ready before heading out. Sinbad and Adara took a roundabout route to the west and began making their way through what might once have been the merchant quarter. Through the windows of the stalls, Sinbad could see items still on display as if the owners had just stepped away moments ago.

"You see, Sinbad, if items like this are here, just ready for the taking, what greater treasures may await us if we can find the ruler's treasure vault?"

"Careful, Adara. Do not let your desire for treasure lead you astray. Until we know more about this town, we must assume doing anything could set off alarms or traps. If there are guardians here, they are well hidden, and I would like them to remain wherever they slumber."

As they turned a corner, Sinbad thought he saw a flash of motion and stopped short, pulling Adara closer. Peeking around the corner again, Sinbad thought he saw a small flash of light just inside a passage leading underground before it disappeared. He motioned for her to stay low and move slowly and then they made their way to the opening. He saw steps descending into the darkness, but the silvery aura of the city gave him just enough illumination to see that the stairs led to a landing below and a passage heading toward the citadel.

Reaching into his pack, Sinbad pulled out a small lamp and lit the wick within. The lantern light cast a pitiful amount of light at street level, but as they descended, it gave him just enough light to ensure he didn't stumble over anything. The passage ran true for several hundred feet until it stopped at a door.

Sinbad quietly lifted the latch and inched the door open to peer within. He could make out a room with a table and chair within, lit by a fire from a fireplace. Overcome with surprise, Sinbad pushed the door open to find an old man sitting in a chair on the opposite side of the room, reading from a large tome.

"Ah, come in. Come in, strangers. It's not often I get visitors here."

Sinbad stared at him in amazement before entering the room. "No, I suppose not."

"What brings you to my humble home?"

"To be honest, I didn't know anyone still lived in Umar? This is a most unexpected surprise."

"I'm certain it is." The old man picked up a small bell and rang it. A beautiful woman appeared from an adjoining room and bowed to Adara and Sinbad. The old man spoke to her in a hushed tone, and she nodded and went back through the door.

"My daughter. We are the last two survivors of Umar. As you might have guessed, there was chaos when the city was cursed, but after the worst had subsided, the citizens banded together to try and survive long enough to escape. Over the years, we have tried many things to escape from the city and several people from the outside found the city, only to be trapped here when it vanished yet again. The centuries were not kind to Umar and now, we, father and daughter, are the last two. When we pass, the history of Umar will be complete."

"Is there nothing you can do now that we are here? If you leave the city now, would you not be saved?"

"No, *effendi*, once you have been taken to the other realm, you are forever bound to the city. Only by lifting the curse, only by destroying the demon stone in the citadel could we rejoin human society. But the stone is said to be indestructible and guarded as well. No, the only advice I have is to flee now while you and your companion can."

"Old man, could you lead us to this stone?"

"What could you, a lone man and woman do that the greatest in Umar were unable to accomplish?"

"Honestly, I do not know. Perhaps nothing. But, if we do not try, then we automatically fail. Do these tunnels lead to the citadel?"

"They do indeed."

"Then if you and your daughter will lead the way, we will accompany you. My crew will be joining me at the Citadel. Once all have gathered, perhaps our combined experiences will provide the clue those who've only known the streets of Umar might have overlooked."

"By Allah, you give me hope, young man. But, if we are to be companions, might I have your name? Old man and young man will become quite tiresome ere too long."

"Of course, where are my manners? I am Sinbad, a sailor and explorer. The young lady here with me is Adara."

"Sinbad and Adara. I am Mehmet and my daughter is Tara. It is a pleasure to meet the two of you. May Allah guide you to a solution to this dilemma. I hope not for myself for I am an old man and have not much longer to live, but my daughter is young and in the prime of her life. It is not right for her to grow old and die alone in this accursed city."

"Allah willing, the two of you will be freed from this curse"

"Come, follow me."

With that, Mehmet motioned for Sinbad and Adara to follow him and he led them down a confusing series of passageways. Sinbad's innate sense of direction told him they were still heading toward the citadel, but he was not convinced this was a faster route than moving overland. Still, Mehmet hadn't given him a reason to doubt his story yet, so he decided to push on as best he could.

After a while, they came to a stone wall. Mehmet moved to the wall and pushed a specific block in with his hand. There was a low rumbling noise and Sinbad watched as the wall swung open as if on a pole, letting them slip past on either side. They appeared to be in a large chamber deep within another building.

Through the dim light, Sinbad could make out the chamber was roughhewn, almost as if it predated the outside buildings. There was a dirt floor and several rows of curved benches surrounding a raised dais in the center of the room. A large black gem floated in mid-air about a foot about the dais. Four huge statues stood at each corner of the dais and Sinbad knew they were guardians set to act if someone approached the dais.

Worst of all, Sinbad stared as large footprints appeared in the dirt floor as if something huge but unseen marched unceasingly around the furthest edge of the benches.

"Mehmet, you might have mentioned some of this before you brought us here."

"I thought it best for you to see it for yourself. The invisible guardian is a fearsome beast that the last priests of Umar raised to defend the black crystal. The curse lies on the crystal. Destroying it would break the curse and banish the guardians, but it is no piece of glass easily broken by simply striking it. One must learn the secret of the crystal first."

Sinbad glared at Mehmet, wishing the old man would speak plainly and not in these infernal riddles. Trying to keep his voice level, he asked, "And where does this secret lie? In some forgotten library in a musty tome?"

Mehmet stroked his white beard and stared at a point somewhere over Sinbad's shoulder. "I do not know for certain, but I believe the crystal will reveal its secrets only to the one meant to destroy it."

Sinbad looked at his partner, but she was keeping her eyes averted. It was unusual for her to remain this quiet this long, but there was no time to decipher yet another mystery. He inched out into the chamber and saw the wall rose about ten feet into the air, but the ceiling was nearly thirty feet. That made this chamber feel like a colosseum more than anything else. He pulled some rope out of his backpack and attached a small grapnel hook to it. Tossing the rope up, he hooked it on the wall and began climbing. As he had suspected, there were more rows of benches up here and aisles leading to four doors. He suspected the citizens of Umar would gather here to witness whatever transpired in the main chamber. He motioned for Adara and Mehmet to use the rope to join him and helped them ascend to the gallery surrounding the chamber.

Once settled, Sinbad pointed to one of the doors. "Remain here. I will go and assemble my crew. Perhaps together we may be able to pierce the mystery of the black crystal."

"Be careful, Sinbad," Adara said in a subdued voice.

Sinbad made his way toward one of the doors, puzzled by Adara's sudden change in demeanor. She seemed as surprised as he had been when they encountered Mehmet, but something about the old man had unsettled her. Still, he needed to concentrate on the issue of the black crystal. Once that was solved, he could worry about her misgivings.

He managed to force one of the bronze doors open and saw it came out on a wide street. Sinbad found suitable items to create a bonfire and dragged the items to as high a point as he could reach. Little by little his crew made their way to the flickering light of the bonfire.

"Taking a bit of a chance there, Sinbad?" Ralf asked as the crew was finally assembled save Haroun and one crewman.

Sinbad quickly recapped what had transpired. While excited by the idea of breaking the curse on Umar, the idea of an invisible guardian, as well as possible stone guardians to defeat threw cold water on their exuberance. After answering a few questions, Sinbad led them inside the building to find Mehmet and Adara watching over the low ledge separating the gallery from the main chamber below.

Mehmet turned to greet the newcomers. Once everyone was introduced, he pointed at the chamber below. "I have been watching the guardian, and I believe it knows we are here. While it may be compelled to complete its circuit around the dais, it pauses longer and longer in front of us. It's almost as if there is an unseen barrier denying it the opportunity to seek us out. If we stay here, we are safe, but I do not know how close we can get before we enter its territory."

Sinbad watched the invisible footprints come quickly from the left and then

" I HAVE BEEN WATCHING THE GUARDIAN..."

slow down and veer toward the group before withdrawing and continuing its trek at a high rate of speed. "If we are to reach our goal we cannot remain here, but how do we fight an invisible foe?"

Rafi held up one hand. "Excuse me, Captain, but I believe I can help here." He rummaged through his medical bag until he came out with two large bottles. "If you remove these tops and throw the contents onto the creature, I believe it will be revealed for all to see."

Henri made a quick motion to ward off evil spirits. "Rafi, I had no idea you dabbled in the dark arts."

"My dear Gaul, I am a physician. I study many things. If there is a way to relieve suffering and cure illnesses, I do not dare look askance at the source. But this is more medical and less magical." He turned to Sinbad. "However, you'll have to be close to the creature to ensure it works."

"If I can see it, I can kill it," Ralf said, lifting his great axe and clapping Sinbad on the shoulder. "Come, Captain, it's time yon fell beast learned to give way to the crew of the *Blue Nymph*."

Rafi showed William and Henri how to best use the bottles, while Sinbad lowered his rope to the chamber below. Carefully, one after the other climbed down to the lower chamber and began moving down the aisles of curved benches toward the dais.

The silence was rendered by an unearthly howl as they approached the closest benches and small puffs of dust rose as the creature could not keep its feet still. Sinbad felt the hair on his arms rise from an unknown static in the air and he knew the barrier—the last line of defense between them and the creature—was about to be breached.

Sinbad waited until the creature revealed its position with a small puff of dust and then swung his arm forward. Both he and Ralf stepped forward, swinging their weapons more to confuse the beast than to contact it, while Henri and William stepped to either side to launch handfuls of Rafi's dust onto the creature. The fine dust exploded into a cloud the second it left their hands and began settling on the invisible creature. Even in the dim light of the chamber, the large human-like body topped with a wolf's head was impossible to miss.

"Be careful, Sinbad, that's a Qutrub," Rafi shouted. Henri and William had drawn their weapons and were trying to flank the creature as Sinbad and Ralf pressed forward. The creature's claw reached out, batting Sinbad's scimitar away while it focused its attention on the large Norseman.

Ralf laughed as the creature pressed closer. "Ah, Beowulf had his Grendel and now I have found a worthy opponent too. One of us will breathe their last today, monster. To the fires of Hell with you."

Sinbad dove in, trying to aid his friend, but the two were so close together, to swing at one was to swing at both. William rushed the creature, but it spun around, sending the man sprawling with a huge swipe of its paw. Herri took a quick shot, but the creature ducked at the last second and the arrow only raised a small line of blood down its shoulder. Sinbad took that as a good sign. *If it bleeds, it can be killed.* He had been afraid only a special weapon could destroy the creature. Another crewman leapt into the fight, but was sent flying into the barrier, dropping senselessly to the ground.

The creature redoubled his attack on Ralf and the two fell to the ground, each holding on to the shaft of Ralf's great axe. Ralf dodged the Qutrub's attempts to bite him and brought his knee up, catching the creature in the stomach. It howled and snapped at Ralf's face, missing by inches. Neither the creature of Ralf could let go of their death grip on the shaft of the weapon for fear of the other gaining control.

Henri was circling around to try and find an angle he could safely take a shot, but the two figures were twisting this way and that to gain an advantage on the other, and he could only mutter Frankish curses in his frustration. William and Tishimi had their weapons at the ready, but the fight was too fluid for either to safely attack the creature without distracting or worse harming their companion.

Suddenly in his other hand, a dark dagger appeared, the weapon warm and throbbing in his hand. "By Allah, you find a most opportune time to reappear. Things must be desperate if you lend your aid unrequested." The black blade merely vibrated in his hand as if urging him into the fray.

Finally, Ralf got his feet underneath the creature and shoved. The Qutrub stumbled backwards, trying to regain its balance when Sinbad's arm moved forward almost on its own, driving the dark blade into the creature's back almost all the way up to the hilt. Sinbad felt an almost fiendish delight as the blade drank deep from the creature's blood.

The Qutrub howled in pain and shock, trying to reach over its shoulder or around its sides to remove the offending blade, but Sinbad, or more precisely, the blade had struck true. Before the creature had time to recover, Ralf stepped forward and with a double-handed swing of his axe, he lopped the creature's head off, sending a spray of black ichor everywhere. The headless corpse slowly crumpled forward and shimmered before turning into a man's form, then a skeleton, and then finally dust. Somewhere, amid the transformation, the dark blade had vanished and Sinbad, once again, was left questioning where it had gone.

Ralf found some of the ichor remaining on the floor and dabbing his fingers in it, drew lines down his cheeks and across his forehead. "Now, that was a fight worth fighting. While I didn't tear his arm off and beat him to death like

Beowulf, it's a rare man indeed who can claim to have slain an ulfhednar."

Rafi came forward and examined Ralf's wounds. "You are feeling well?"

"I am fine. Mere scratches. I don't know what that magic powder you used, physician, but it was powerful stuff. What do you call it?"

"Talcum powder."

The entire group stopped motionless and almost as one turned their heads toward the older man. Henri finally found his voice and squeaked out what was on everyone's mind. "*Talcum powder?!*"

"Well, yes. You don't think I carry powders to turn invisible creatures visible around like it was a stomach curative? I'm a doctor, not a wizard. I knew the talcum powder would create enough of a cloud that wherever it settled, the creature would be revealed."

"You risked our lives with talcum powder?" Henri squawked before Tishmi grabbed him by the arm and escorted him away.

Rafi looked at Sinbad with surprise. "Really. These young people always want to make things more complicated than needed. Would you use a gold piece to buy something if copper would do? No. So, why would I use a powerful powder, if I even had one, when a simple process would do?"

Sinbad made consoling gestures at Rafi, who was giving Henri dark looks. "You've done nothing wrong, Rafi. The creature was slain, and our path is clear. You know Henri."

Rafi continued muttering things about young people as he repacked everything in his medical kit and Sinbad ensured everyone was no worse the wear before they began moving toward the dais. Everyone's weapons were at the ready, but even as they reached the stairs, the stone statues did not move. Either there *were* simply statues, or perhaps something else was required to activate them. There was no time to find out though, so Sinbad positioned his crew to alert him and intercept any of the statues that might begin moving.

Approaching the dais, Sinbad and the others saw the strange black gem floated inches above the surface of the pedestal. Even though the room was dimly lit, and the gem appeared to be completely opaque, there still seemed to be a strange light within, sensed more than seen.

The company examined the strange gem from differing angles before Sinbad turned back to Mehmet. "So, the gem is said to be indestructible?"

"Try it for yourself."

Sinbad knew Mehmet would never speak so casually if there was any chance he was wrong, but apparently Ralf took that as a challenge. Before Sinbad could stop him, the giant warrior raised his axe and brought it down on the gem. A burst of force shot out in all directions, throwing those on the dais down the stairs to the floor of the chamber. Sinbad picked himself up, shaking the cobwebs out of his head. One by one, his crew made their way to their feet and Ralf hung his head, not in shame of attempting to break the gem, but because he had failed.

"Next time, let's talk our options through before we just try to break a gem possibly holding a curse within its form," Sinbad said, as he moved up to the pedestal again. True to Mehmet's words, there was not a scratch on the gem from Ralf's titanic blow. "Well, we now know that brute force won't work. Any other suggestions."

Tishimi moved closer and began running her hand along the gem, feeling the pattern of the facets as well as visually examining them. She had William move a torch closer. The gem greedily devoured the light faster than it could illuminate the surface. Finally, she turned to Sinbad. "There are no flaws. I do not believe there is a jeweler in the world who could find an appropriate spot to try and split the gem in two. So, neither blunt nor precise force will affect this stone."

"So, we're stymied? Is there no way to break this stone open?" Henri asked.

"A stone that perfectly cut does present a problem, but there may be a solution," Rafi said, running his hand through his beard. "I've seen fakirs use sound to break things. Mostly to shatter glass, but if the sound could be directed, it might affect even the mightiest of stones."

William scoffed. "Unfortunately, I left my bagpipes in my other outfit."

Before an argument could break out, Mehmet stepped forward, his eyes alight. "*Effendis*, would a tuning fork possibly help?"

"You have such a devise, Mehmet?" Sinbad asked, his curiosity and his caution raised by this sudden revelation.

"Sinbad, I was not always alone in this city. I've simply outlived everyone but my daughter. Along with my studies, I used to amuse myself studying music . . . more on the mathematical progressions than for the purity of music itself. My daughter is more musically inclined than I, but I enjoyed building instruments for her entertainment, especially when she was young. Still, designing a tuning fork was child's play with the right tools. Perhaps one of them might suit the purposes your physician prescribed?"

"Where are these devices? Surely you don't have any on you?" Henri asked.

"Of course not, don't be foolish. However, my home is not far from here. Your captain found it easily enough. I can be there and back while you rest and recover from your fight against the guardian."

Sinbad started at the gem and then back at the old man. He suspected there was more to this than what Mehmet was saying, but without more evidence, he couldn't turn down a possible solution. "Go, Mehmet. We will await your return."

The crew gathered around the dais, examining the pedestal and the gem from various angles. Henri prodded and poked at the pedestal, as if searching for a hidden switch, while Ralf and William debated whether a mace might be more effective on a gem if a blade failed. Tishimi, as was her custom, kept her counsel to herself and stood back from the main group, watching the surrounding areas with a wary eye.

"What do you think, Captain?" Henri asked, as he pushed one last protrusion without any luck. "Do you think that crazy old man has any idea what he's talking about?"

Sinbad paused before answering, looking at the entrance Mehmet had disappeared through "I don't know, Henri, but I know I don't have any answers for this problem at the moment. I'm up for trying just about anything *if* it doesn't seem too dangerous."

"But jumping in to tackle an unseen foe?" Ralf asked before letting out a loud laugh. "No, that's not dangerous at all."

"I admit it wasn't optimal, but then again, Ralf, it's not like we haven't fought unseen beings before. At least this one wasn't flying."

The giant man laughed again before responding. "True, true, but don't go looking to make things more difficult than they already are by inviting Allah to up the stakes just to satisfy your love of danger."

"Me? Love danger?"

"Only slightly less than you love treasure . . . or women."

The rest of the crew razzed their captain for a bit and then fell back into various conversations while they awaited Mehmet's return. Sinbad noted that Adara hadn't joined in though and moved over to where she stood on the periphery of the milling bodies.

"You seem to have fallen into a foul mood ever since we met Mehmet. Is there something wrong?"

Adara shook as if rousing herself from a daydream before turning to face Sinbad. "I'm sorry. It's just we've gone from treasure hunt to a rescue mission. I was just surprised at the sudden change in our plans."

"Oh, it's still a treasure hunt, but if we can rescue Mehmet and his daughter from the trap of a city they've lived their whole lives in . . . why, is that not just another treasure?" Sinbad lifted an arm in a sweeping motion, moving in a circle about him. "Looking at this city, I have no doubts there are treasures just waiting to be scooped up. The few buildings we've investigated tell me this was a wildly prosperous city in its day. Even if we can only leave with everyday items, I know they'll bring a fine price in the marketplace. It might take a little longer to gain the value we would have secured from gems or gold, it's all still valuable to the right collector."

"Collectors? Hmm."

"Now, see, there you go getting all quiet again. I thought you wanted adventure? Isn't that why you came?"

Adara smiled at Sinbad before replying. "This whole trip has been one big adventure. I must admit, so far, it has been nothing like I imagined."

Sinbad chuckled a bit before smiling back. "Guilty as charged. For some reason, Allah has placed in me a craving for excitement. Treasures? They're simply the by-product of seeking out opportunities wherever they lead me."

Out of the corner of his eye, he saw Mehmet and his daughter appear and several of the crewmen ceased their banter as Tara approached. Her almost unearthly beauty caught the gaze of one and all as she stood next to her father with her head bowed.

"You were successful, Mehmet?"

"Indeed, I was, Sinbad. My daughter found my tuning instruments. If one does not work, we can certainly try the others."

"Tara, your father tells me you are quite the musician. Do you have any theories on which we should try first?"

"I have been told, though never actually seen, a singer's voice can shatter glass if the right note is struck and held long enough. It usually requires a higher-than-normal pitch, so I suggest starting with the highest-pitched tuning fork and working our way down. If that does not work, then perhaps different forks struck at the same time might create a disharmonious wave which could have the desired effect."

"That makes perfect sense."

The crew fell to, helping Mehmet arrange the tuning instruments on one of the benches. Sinbad noticed neither Mehmet nor Tara actually stepped on the dais while they were working. Sinbad was about to ask Mehmet about that, but the old man interrupted with a statement of his own.

"Sinbad, this is why you and your crew are a most welcome sight. Even if Tara and I could have defeated the guardian, it would have done no good. No one from Umar can step on the dais, nor can anything one born of Umar actually affect the gem. If you were to find a way to remove it from the pedestal and hand it to me, it would just go through my hands as if they were made of clouds. Only someone from outside this cursed city can release the inhabitants, else we would have broken the seal and returned to the real-world centuries ago."

"I see, Mehmet. Whomever cursed this city was oddly specific, but then again, if the city only appears for so many nights every hundred years, the odds someone from outside the city finding the source of the curse and destroying it before the deadline was a reasonable precaution."

Mehmet's eyes flashed with a hidden fire before he answered. "Yes, the trap was cunning. I have no doubts the original inhabitants rained curses down on he who bound this city to its cycle." But, as swiftly as the storm clouds had seemingly gathered around Mehmet, his face brightened, and he handed Sinbad a large tuning fork. "But, with the day of our release so close, why should I spend time angry at that which happened so long ago. Please, Sinbad, release us from this curse."

Sinbad carefully took the tuning fork from the old man and climbed the dais. Striking the edge of the fork against the pedestal, he held the fork near the gem, but there was no apparent reaction. He moved the fork around, over, under, and beside the gem, but either the note was wrong, or it wasn't powerful enough.

Fork after fork was tried but after going through the entire series, there was no appreciable change to the enigmatic gem. If anything, the darkness seemed to become deeper, as if the gem was mocking their feeble efforts.

Taking a short break to rest and refresh, the crew took up the challenge by trying different combinations of the forks. Every pair, trio, and other combination was tried over the next few hours. Finally, Sinbad directed everyone in the crew to pick up one or two of the forks and strike them simultaneously and as hard as they could. The cacophony was tremendous, but as the crew moved closer, the gem began to react. Flakes began appearing on the surface and visible fissures formed, releasing a foul gas into the air.

"Quickly, again." Sinbad cried, clacking the two forks he held against each other to renew the vibrations.

Under the sonic assault of all the forks, the gems face fractured and then chunks began to break away.

"Yes, yes. Just a bit more," Mehmet cried as strange black light shot into the air from deep within the gem.

Just as the gem was about to crumble, Tara suddenly shouted. "No, stop! You don't know what you're releasing." However, before she could finish her protest, the gem erupted, sending a spray of shards throughout the room, wounding many of the crew. Sinbad felt the shards cutting deeply into his face and chest. Before he could react, he heard a roar from behind him and then the floor dropped away, sending the crew careening down into the darkness. He tried to grab ahold of anything, but there was no time, and the floor came up to meet him with a sickening thud.

Sinbad woke to the feeling of water dripping on his face. Feeling as if the *Blue Nymph* had been dropped on him, he forced his eyes open to see his crew chained to the walls surrounding him. He found the strength to rise off the floor where he had been laying and rushed over to his crew. To his relief, he found each of them had a strong pulse and were breathing regularly.

Now assured of the crew's health, Sinbad took in the room. It appeared to be a standard dungeon cell with straw in one corner and a small bucket off to the other side tucked behind a small outcropping from the natural rock around them. He looked around and saw that their weapons had been confiscated and were hung with care on the wall just beyond the barred door, taunting the prisoners.

"How do you like your new accommodations, Sinbad?" asked a booming voice. It was familiar but not. Sinbad held his tongue, waiting for this tormentor to show themselves before giving them the satisfaction of a response.

A large, swarthy being floated down the hall. It snapped its fingers and the torches in the hall flared to life. The face was familiar but not, but the sense of arrogance coming from the being was very familiar to Sinbad. He'd dealt with beings like this before and had no love for what was to come next.

"What, no words for me, Sinbad? After all, I am most gracious for you freeing me from the curse of Umar. You cannot imagine how many nights I have waited for this moment; the moment I can flee this city and return to my rightful place. Please, do not be petulant, Sinbad. This is a night for celebration."

"You make quite free use of my name, demon."

The being laughed, which did nothing to make its face any pleasanter. "Why should I not, Sinbad? After all, did you not willingly tell me who you were?"

Suddenly Sinbad put it together. "Mehmet?"

"That was the name I used then, and it will do now. After all, I'm certain my original name would mean nothing to you. After being trapped here for over five hundred years, I doubt any but the most erudite of sages would recognize it."

The being turned translucent and then flowed through the bars of the door to materialize in the cell. "Come, Sinbad. I could not have done this without you. I spoke truly, none from Umar could have released me. After all, I was forbidden to approach the gem and the original inhabitants all perished centuries ago."

"And Tara?"

"A peri. I lured her here centuries ago and she has been my handmaiden ever since. However, she will not be visiting you. Her futile act of defiance is being dealt with. Luckily, Adara is made of stronger stuff. Then again, the ifrit love how easily you mortal men are twisted into doing what they want."

Sinbad lunged at the floating creature without thinking but found himself completely immobilized and hanging in mid-air, his fingers inches from the creature's throat. "We'll see how well things can be twisted, demon," he managed to whisper through his frozen jaw.

The creature pouted and floated back beyond Sinbad's grasp. "Now, is that any way to treat your benefactor. After all, I sent Adara to find you. Why she agreed to help me . . . well, I'll let her explain."

"I thought you said you couldn't leave the city. Would that not apply to any who were from Umar?"

The demonic creature preened. "I knew you had a sharp mind, Sinbad. While it was true Tara couldn't leave the city after spending time in the other realm, this *is* the first time Adara has been to Umar. Well, again I'll let her explain. It would be wrong to tell her story for her. Besides, I'm enjoying having you here, Sinbad. It is so unsatisfying how the lesser beings bow and scrape before me. Djinni, ifriti, peri, marid . . . so tiny, so fragile."

Sinbad found the creature's statement curious in spite of himself. "You are no Djinn?"

The creature laughed and grew to a size that nearly filled the cell. "I am a jann. The janni were created to rule over lesser beings. However, most were defeated centuries ago and banished to places like this. Humans and spirits combined their magics and their treacherous cunning to betray their betters. No, Sinbad, I'm no being here to grant a few wishes or to trick a lost traveler. I will take my rightful place in Arabia. I shall raise armies of fell beings and I will remind both spirits and humans where they truly fall in the order of things."

"If you were defeated once, you can be again."

The jann laughed. "Bold words for a mortal, but then again, I knew you were a man who loved a challenge the moment I laid eyes on you." Before Sinbad could ask the obvious question, Mehmet went on. "I may not have been able to physically escape this city, but my magic, while greatly weakened, was not so bound. Creating a scrying pool was child's play and even though Umar was unable to be seen by the mortal world, its secrets were made clear to me. I have followed your many voyages, Sinbad. I knew if there was one man clever and brave enough to free me . . . with the right incentives, of course . . . it would have to be you."

Sinbad felt the constriction of his limbs subside and he crumpled to the floor before he could catch himself. Easing back to his feet, he turned to face the jann. "If you have followed my voyages, you should know I'll never stop trying to defeat you."

"And I would be most disappointed if you did. For a mortal, you are a worthy opponent, Sinbad. However, I am just below the gods themselves. You have no

"...HE TURNED TO FACE THE JANN..."

chance to defeat me fully armed and equipped. How are you going to do that with your bare hands?"

"When I discover that, you'll be the second to know."

"I look forward to the challenge, Sinbad. But I must leave you now." The jann snapped his fingers and the manacles holding his crew sprang open and they tumbled to the ground. "Stop looking so concerned. They're merely asleep. I have even healed their wounds as I healed yours. Although," he paused, and a sinister grin settled on his face. "you may wish I had left you all asleep for eternity once you face what's ahead."

Before Sinbad could speak, the jann disappeared. Sinbad quickly moved to his crew and started waking them up. Just as the last one had started to come to, there was a soft cough at the cell door. Sinbad turned to see a being standing there. It was human-shaped but wreathed in fire, but there was no question it was a feminine shape.

"Sinbad?"

"Adara?"

It was hard to read the expressions on Adara's face, but Sinbad noted hints of remorse. She stood just beyond his reach, staring at him. The other crew members withdrew to the far end of their cell, giving them the illusion of privacy.

"Why did you do this, Adara?"

"A motive as old as time, Sinbad. Revenge."

Sinbad stepped back and looked closely at Adara. "Revenge? But I've never met you before. I think I would have remembered you in either shape."

"You did meet me, though there was no way for you to know. Do you remember when you raided Sheik Ahmed's camp?"

A smile spread across Sinbad's face before he replied. "That slaver? Yes, I remember. We freed over fifty slaves in that raid and helped ourselves to quite a treasure to reward ourselves for our troubles." He paused for a moment, mentally remembering that raid. His crew swept over the slaver's camp, scattering the guards and cutting the ropes to the tents, catching the sleeping men in the heavy fabric. The fight was over almost before the slavers knew what had happened. Sinbad cocked his head to one side, looking even closer at Adara. "Were you among the slaves?"

Adara shook her head, glancing down at the floor. "Not in the way you were thinking. Do you remember a large orange gem mounted on a scepter."

"Indeed, I do. The caliph of Khorasan gave me quite the price when I sold it to him."

The ifritta bristled and her posture changed, standing ramrod straight and glaring at Sinbad. She didn't bother hiding the distain in her voice. "Indeed, and he would have paid much more because he recognized what you did not. I was a slave to the gem. You took me from the sheik and turned me over to one who knew how to summon me. He forced me to do unspeakable things until his nephew overthrew him."

Her visage changed, becoming almost feral as she relived those memories. Unconsciously her fingers turned into claws and her flame burned bright enough to force Sinbad to take several steps back. "In that battle, the scepter was broken and the gem shattered, freeing me to seek revenge on the two people I hated most in the world, the caliph . . . and you. The caliph's burned body was discovered by his nephew the night of his triumph. He assumed the caliph had accidentally burnt to death. Being unaware of my existence, he did not seek me out—which saved his life. With the gem destroyed and the caliph dead, the only one left who could have known of my existence was you. I could not take the chance you would try to enslave me, so you had to be destroyed. Destroyed, but in a manner that would never lead back to me."

"How could you hold me responsible for that which I did not know?"

"The things that happened while I was a prisoner of that madman would have driven anyone to an unreasonable rage. I swore no human would ever be my master again and the fact you had sold the scepter to the caliph made me believe you knew I was in the gem. So, when Zophir reached out to me and told me of his scheme, it seemed the perfect way to get my revenge on you."

"Zophir?"

"The one you know as Mehmet. His true name is Zophir. Though that knowledge will do you no good. He is not easily summoned nor bound like a djinn or an ifrit."

"Do you know what he intends?"

"It's a very simple plan. He intends to leave the city tomorrow and leave you and your crew behind. Without the gem to anchor it, when the city disappears with the setting of the full moon it will never return from the twilight realm where it rests."

"And you willingly agreed to this?"

She looked down at the floor before finally responding. "I did . . . at first. But, as I have come to know you during our journey together, I realized how foolish I had been. In my anger and despair, I had made an agreement I was bound to complete because a contract with a jann is not to be disobeyed. At least, not without consequences, as Tara is discovering."

"Is exposing Zophir's plan to me not disobeying him?"

Adara glanced around and moved closer to the cell door, lowering her voice. "Perhaps, but I suspect he intends to leave me here in the city along with you. The djinni and ifriti are but ants in his vision."

Sinbad looked around the cell and outside of the possible reappearance of Grachene, that untrustworthy present from the Goddess of the Underworld, they were helpless to defend themselves against anything the Jann intended, which included simply ignoring them until the deadline. He thought of a half-dozen options and tossed them just as quickly. He was about to canvass the crew for ideas when he stopped and turned back to Adara.

"Did he forbid you to release us from this cell?"

"He has not spoken to me since you fell through the chamber's floor to this pit, so the short answer is no."

"Can you open the door?"

"There are no keys visible, but to a being such as me, that is not an issue. Step away, Sinbad, lest you be injured."

Sinbad moved away from the cell door as the ifritta put her hands on the bars above and below the lock. Her hands glowed with a hellish light and the metal began to glow cherry red before flowing like water beneath her touch. She moved to the other set of bars and repeated the same process, allowing the lock to simply crash to the floor with nothing to support it.

Sinbad motioned for his crew to follow him, and they made their way out of the cell and secured the weapons hanging across the hall. Tishimi set the three blades on the floor in front of her and knelt with her legs tucked beneath her. She placed her hands on the scabbards and spoke soft words while keeping her eyes closed. Only after she had finished, did she carefully set the blades into their usual places on her waist before rising. The others had finished inspecting their weapons before clustering around Sinbad.

He held up his hands to halt the tumult of questions and faced his benefactor. "Adara, do you know where Tara is?"

"I do. But shouldn't we flee before it's too late?"

"That would be the logical thing to do, yes. But Tara tried to warn us before the gem was destroyed. Therefore, I cannot in good conscience abandon her."

He stopped, then continued softly. "I'm convinced Zophir did not destroy us outright because he has not regained his whole strength. So, it would be better to fight him now than let him escape into the wide world, where he will have time to recover and summon allies. This may be an impossible battle, but it may be our only chance."

Adara shook her head, "No, Sinbad. Think about what you're saying. You have no great mages amongst your crew. You are mortals going against something that makes a Djinn pale by comparison. What can you do?"

"We can try and that will have to be enough. Better to make him kill us than spend eternity trapped in this twilight realm you mentioned."

"I think you're a fool, Sinbad. But then again, I must be a greater fool because

I know what you're up against and I intend to fight by your side."

Henri gave her a dirty look. "As if we could trust you."

Adara turned to the Frenchman and the flames on her head turned from reddish orange to a bluish white, driving the crew back with the sudden heat. "Trust me or not, mortal. I remain unless you think you can make me leave."

Sinbad stepped between the two. "Henri, we need all the allies we can get. If she proves false, we'll deal with her then. Otherwise, we are wasting time." He turned back to Adara, whose hair was slowly subsiding along with the anger in her eyes. "Adara, can you show us the way?"

"Who is more foolish? The fool or the one who follows him?" she said, mostly to herself before motioning down the hall. "This way."

The crew made their way through a maze of passageways. Some of the hallways sported doors that hung open. Pausing, the crew could see the rooms were filled with gems, gold, ornate furniture, and priceless paintings. It was all they could do to resist stopping and filling their pockets with the treasures, but Adara kept urging them onward.

After the fifth or sixth room passed, Henri balked at her urging. "And why should we not help ourselves to a bit of treasure? I'd rather die a rich man than a poor one."

"Because none of that is real. Perhaps you see those things as valuable items, but to my eyes, those rooms are filled with spikes, crawling animals, and pits. Those rooms were set there to lure the unwary to their dooms. If you step within, you'll almost certainly never step out."

Henri pulled his hand back away from the door as if it had suddenly developed a snapping mouth. "But it looks so real."

"Djinni know the hearts of men. Again, I do not see it as you do, but I suspect if one was to describe what lies within, without being influenced by the others, you'd each describe the contents differently."

Rafi sighed deeply and then raised his eyes toward the ceiling. "Is such magic even possible? Can one not even trust his own eyes?"

Sinbad clapped the physician on the shoulder. "Perhaps, Allah has granted you this knowledge now to protect you when we face the jann later."

"Perhaps. Or perhaps he enjoys vexing me."

"Now, you sound like Omar. I'll have to tell him that when we meet him on the ship." Sinbad shook his head and laughed at the memory of his long-suffering friend before motioning the crew forward in Adara's wake. Armed with the knowledge of the traps awaiting them, the crew still examined the rooms as they passed them but now with a wary eye instead of a greedy one.

After another series of twisting passages, they came to a long hallway lined with doors and a double door made of brass at the end. Adara pointed ahead.

"Tara lies just beyond those doors. We'll have to be careful. Zophar has not paid attention to you up till now, but once we enter, we'll be invading one of his sanctums. We'll have to move quickly before he arrives."

Sinbad motioned and the crew spread out, moving down the hall in pairs, weapons at the ready. They had just about reached the halfway point when the hallway doors sprang open, disgorging skeletons armed with ancient swords. Momentarily caught off guard, the crew was forced backward away from their goal before they rallied. Ralf forced his way forward, using his great axe as a battering ram, shoving several of the skeletons backward and creating some space for his companions to act. William stepped up and swung his sword, lopping off one of the skeleton's arms, sending bones and a rusty sword clattering. Tishimi blocked a clumsy strike with her wakizashi before cutting down, severing the skeleton's head and right arm from its body. To everyone's horror, the skeleton warrior continued its assault on the samurai, seemingly unbothered by losing a quarter of its body.

Henri was forced to abandon any thought of using his bow as the skeletal warriors pressed in quickly. He and Sinbad wove a web of steel at the rear of the group, fending off one attack while delivering crippling blows of their own. Seeing some of his crewmen struggling against the press of warriors, Sinbad slipped through a gap leaving Henri to hold the rear. Ralf war cries were heard over the melee as he quickly shifted from using the axe to block an attack to swinging it almost scythe-like to shatter the bones of his opponents.

It took longer than Sinbad would have liked, but any parts left intact continued to attack until they were rendered incapable of movement. It took the crew pulverizing the skeletal warriors into dust before they felt safe enough to continue. A glance inside one of the doors showed a simple room, only a few feet in width or length—just enough room to fit one skeletal warrior and their weapon. From the accumulated dust, Sinbad deduced they had been set here years ago. He was unsure whether their mere presence or if they had stepped on a trigger. Either way, they would have to be more alert for other potential traps. It would do no one any good if they were stopped before they had their final encounter with Zophar.

Reaching the chamber at the end of the hall, the crew was taken aback, seeing the peri trapped within a huge amber crystal suspended on chains hanging from the ceiling. The crystal was centered over a burning brazier and dark, oily smoke swirled up to mingle with the smoke coming from the torches ensconced along the walls. The only break in the walls was an open doorway showing a darkened hallway leading deeper into the bowels of the city. To Sinbad, this scene reminded him of several torture chambers he'd had the unpleasant experiences to witness, and he could taste the bile of those memories in the back of his throat.

It appeared that she slumbered within, but Sinbad could see little flinches and contortions on her skin. Whatever was going on within the crystal, he knew the quicker they freed her, the better.

Ralf approached the center of the room and went to move the brazier but stopped. "Darn thing is bolted into the floor here. Anyone see any tools lying around?"

Sinbad looked over at Adara. "I'm guessing if we were to put the fire out, that would alert Zophar?"

"I do not know. Nothing in this room looks suspicious, but the jann's magic dwarfs mine. I am inclined to agree with you, though. Perhaps we could lower her from mid-air and move her prison somewhere we could examine it closer?"

"A sound idea. Henri, William, Ralf, try to see if there is a way to loosen the chains suspending the crystal. There's not much we can do with her ten feet over our head. Rafi, prepare your medical supplies. I don't know if a Peri heals the same as a human, but we should render whatever aid that we can."

The crew members fell to and eventually Henri found the device to lower the crystal from its current position toward the ground. Standing on either side of the brazier, the rest of the crew grabbed the crystal prison and lowered it gently to the ground. The amber crystal seemed to be seamless and there was no visible cavity. It was almost as if the crystal had been molded around her body.

The first mate finally rose to his feet after one last examination of the crystal. "It's no use, Sinbad. There's nothing we can do for her here with the limited tools we have."

Sinbad laughed, "Ralf, you're a genius."

The Norseman looked at him in confusion. "Thank you, I think."

"Unless the jann created this crystal whole cloth out of magic, then it was obviously not created in this small room." He pointed to the other exit. "Come, there must be a workshop nearby."

Tishimi took point with Adara who tried to spot any illusions. The rest of the crew lifted the amber crystal to their shoulders and followed the two women down the dark hallway. It was hard to say how far they had walked, but eventually, they spotted a light ahead and came out into a huge room. At the center of the room was a large boiling cauldron. Flames of different colors flickered at its base and above it, a slow drip of an amber substance fed the cauldron.

Looking around the room, the crew was taken aback by the sight of hundreds of crystals similar to the one they had just carried in. On closer inspection, the crystals contained the macabre remains of human skeletons—men, women, and even children—entombed within the crystals.

A righteous fire grew in Sinbad's stomach. Any thought of simply fleeing flew from his mind. "By Allah, what kind of unholy beast have we set free? It is one thing to fight a worthy foe, but to make war on women and children? No, this affront must not go unavenged."

Even Adara seemed upset by the gruesome discovery. "Sinbad, I may have been blinded in my rage, but I swear I knew nothing of this. This is beyond the pale. We must discover a way to free Tara. Perhaps she knows something that might prove helpful."

Ripping his eyes away from the horror around him, Sinbad directed the crew to set Tara's prison down near a bench and then began scouring the cauldron room for anything that might prove useful. Several tools were spotted and rejected for potentially being more dangerous to Tara than the crystal.

"Sinbad, I believe I've found something," Rafi called motioning with one arm to the rest of the group. They rushed over and saw Rafi had discovered a set of tuning forks hidden beneath several bolts of cloth.

"Perhaps what works on one gem may work on another," the physician quipped as he started handing out the forks to the crowd gathered around him.

"It's certainly worth a shot," Henri said, grabbing one in each hand. Armed with the forks, the crew returned to Tara's prison and took up spots surrounding the amber crystal. Once everyone was positioned, Sinbad slowly lifted his forks above the crystal and then brough them down quickly, clinging the metal against the gleaming stone.

The cacophony was deafening, but the prison shattered almost instantaneously, depositing Tara amidst a pile of amber shards. The crew carefully picked her up and laid her on a nearby table while Rafi secured his medical equipment. He gave her an examination and then brought out a small jar carefully sealed with wax. Motioning for everyone to move back, he broke the seal and then carefully lifted one edge of the lid directly below her nose.

Even at a distance, the crew began coughing and gagging from the smell wafting from the jar. Sinbad couldn't imagine how this was supposed to help the peri, but he thanked Allah a thousand times Rafi had never felt the need to subject him to that particular ministration. After a few seconds, the peri's eyes shot open, and Rafi snapped the jar shut and stepped out of Tara's striking range. The peri sat up and then emptied her stomach, while Rafi quickly applied a fresh coat of wax to the jar and set it back inside his medical kit.

"By the gods, old man, were you trying to help me or finish me off?' Tara snarled once her stomach had stopped trying to turn inside out.

"You're welcome," Rafi said, glancing over his shoulder at her. "I'd avoid eating anything for about four hours. Probably wouldn't end well."

"If I had my way, you would not end well either . . . but thank you."

William stepped over and assisted Tara from the table. Once steady on her feet, William led her over to where the crew was examining the room. Sinbad wasted no time in questioning her. "Tara, can you tell us what happened here? When Zophar told us the original inhabitants had died, is this what he meant."

The peri glanced around; her features etched in sorrow. "I was not an original inhabitant of this cursed city, so all I know is what he told me. Apparently, he was allied with the ruler of this city when it was a major trade city, years before the desert swallowed this region. He used to laugh and say he was the shadow behind the throne. No matter what the viziers and chamberlains thought, Zophar had the final word with the ruling emir."

Tara glanced up at the rows and rows of crystals embedded in the walls surrounding the gigantic workshop. "He never said exactly what happened. When the city was cursed, he found himself not only cut off from his major sources of power, but also bound here eternally, I believe it drove him mad. He forced the inhabitants to attempt to break the black gem, not realizing they couldn't approach the dais any more than he could. Many of them died in the attempts and many others died in the revolt against him shortly afterward. Finally, he slew all the remaining inhabitants just to remove their irritating presence. He embalmed all of them in these crystals—some already dead, some doomed to die a slow, lingering death."

"Wait, so you don't die when you're put into the crystals?" Rafi said, a horrified look on his face.

"No, treacherous doctor, you are rendered immobile and unconscious. You have no knowledge of any passage of time, no hunger and no need to breathe. You feel no pain. The body simply dies little by little over time. A merciful death, Zophar called it."

Sinbad glanced around and his voice took on a menacing tone. "There is nothing merciful about a death like that. But you give me an idea, Tara. Obviously, this crystal affects both elementals as well as humans."

"I am living proof of that, Captain."

"Would this affect the jann?"

"That I cannot swear to. The jann is a higher being than one such as myself or Adara. However, since it was created by him, unless he specifically ensured against that, it is a magic of the highest power."

Sinbad motioned his crew closer. "I do not know how long we have, but I have an idea. Follow my lead and perhaps we'll leave this city with both its treasures and our lives.

Hours later, Zophar floated into the workshop to find Sinbad sitting in a chair in the middle of the hellscape that was the workshop. Torches burned from every sconce and there were extra torches gathered from other rooms arranged to ensure the light reflected off the macabre amber coffins lining the walls of the room. Sinbad languorously rose to his feet and bowed derisively toward the jann.

"Ah, there you are, Zophar. I was afraid I would have to go hunting for you."

The jann's booming voice jarred Sinbad, even as he was braced for it. "Oh ho, little mouse. I didn't expect to find you here. I was positive when I found you had escaped your cell that you would have fled the city posthaste. Imagine my surprise at seeing no sign of you anywhere on the outskirts of the city and then even more surprise discovering that traitorous peri's body gone missing. I admit she was angelic in appearance, but I never took you for a grave robber, Sinbad."

"Then you did *not* spend enough time scrying on me, Jann. I have recovered treasures from tombs and catacombs from all the seven seas. I've never found the wisdom in burying treasures with the dead. They have either gone on to paradise or to Hell and in neither place would those things be useful. But why do you speak of Tara in the past tense?"

The jann paused and cocked his head to one side. "Well now, it seems I have underestimated you, Sinbad. Have you truly freed the peri?"

"Perhaps, but you're still missing the big picture here."

"The audacity of how you speak to your betters, Sinbad, is all that is keeping you alive. You amuse me, so speak quickly before I grow bored and destroy you."

"Zophar, you stand here in the midst of your greatest sins. You betrayed your city and the people therewithin. It is time to face your judgement."

The jann drew itself up straight and began growing, rising to almost twelve feet in height. "You insignificant flea. You, mortal, presume to preach to me of my sins and believe you are in a position to render judgement against me?"

"I do. As captain of the *Blue Nymph*, I am the highest-ranking surviving mortal within this city and I speak for those who cannot," Sinbad said, swinging one of his arms in a large arc encompassing the amber crystals surrounding the room. "It falls to me to speak for those who cannot give voice to their cries for vengeance and justice. Jann, it is time you paid for your crimes."

Sinbad had to dive to one side to avoid a bolt of lightning that struck where he had been standing. As he rolled back up to his feet, the jann began advancing slowly, its murderous eyes locked on his smaller form.

"No, you insignificant worm, it is time you and your crew join those who adorn Umar's walls. Perhaps in a few thousand years, the curse will be permanently lifted and scholars those years hence will find your living casket."

"Come and face me in honest combat, you son of a div."

Another bolt of energy sought out Sinbad and he barely managed to avoid it by diving backwards. He gave ground slowly, his weapon at the ready and he motioned with the tip of his blade for the jann to come and fight.

With a roar, the jann materialized a huge scimitar out of thin air and rushed toward Sinbad. Just as he reached the spot where Sinbad had been sitting, the cauldron, which had been raised to near the ceiling of the room, suddenly tipped forward, spilling out a tidal wave of amber. Before the jann could react, he was engulfed and swept off his feet in the amber fluid.

The rest of the crew, hidden in the rafters continued to pull on the ropes, dumping more and more of the amber fluid onto the floor. Sinbad scrambled to reach the prepositioned high ground of crates and tables. The tables shook as the fluid covered the entirety of the workshop in several feet of the fluid.

There was an inarticulate scream and then the jann lay on his back completely covered over by the rapidly cooling and hardening fluid. Sinbad called out that he was safe and for the rest of the crew to remain where they were until the liquid cooled.

The jann struggled against the cloying liquid and they saw cracks forming around its body, but they were quickly filled in as the liquid continued to pour out of the cauldron. Finally, Sinbad saw the jann's eyes droop forward as the soporific effects of the crystal amber took effect and the only sound was the hissing of the remnants of the amber cooling as they dripped from the upturned cauldron.

Sinbad waited impatiently, but better a few more minutes of inactivity versus a lifetime if the amber wasn't solid enough to hold their weight. Finally, the amber settled into a dull orange and Sinbad gingerly climbed down to the new floor. Satisfied it would hold his weight; he called for his crew to join him.

Adara came to him in a rush. "Sinbad, the hour is drawing late. If we do not flee the city soon, there may not be another chance."

He turned to the peri who was being helped by William and Henri. "Tara, do you know the shortest route from here to the edge of the city."

"I do. Please follow me. If I am delaying you too much, please leave me behind. Save yourselves."

William swept her up in his arms. "That'll be enough of that, lass. You just direct. I'll take care of the runnin'."

With that, the crew took off at a steady, but hurried pace. Tara directed them past several obvious exit routes, explaining the jann had built them to lure the unwary into traps. Finally, the crew rushed out of a building into a wide boulevard as the sun was no more than a hand's width above the horizon.

" JANN, IT IS TIME YOU PAID FOR YOUR CRIMES."

Recognizing a couple of the landmarks, Sinbad sent his men hurrying as fast as they could toward the edge of the city.

"Sinbad, have you seen any signs of Haroun?" Ralf called as they rushed away from the town center.

"Not since we originally split up. Since he was not in the cell we found ourselves in, I can only presume the jann couldn't find him either. Let us hope he'll be at the camp and that he had better luck than we did."

Tara called out, "Past the second building, turn to the left. There is a street that will take you to a side gate."

The crew redoubled their efforts and soon the gate was in sight. The sun was sinking ever lower, sending deepening shadows across the streets. The crew was only a few dozen feet short of the gate when a group of men stepped out of the shadows, forming a human barrier just inside the gate, weapons drawn."

"Halt in the name of the emir."

The crew skidded to a stop several feet short of their goal. "Of all the times for . . . Sinbad, what should we do?" Ralf asked, readying his axe.

There was a sudden flurry of movement along the top of the wall and archers appeared, aiming their shafts at the trapped crew. Sinbad held out his hands and then motioned for his crew to carefully put their weapons away. Moving with all deliberation, he stepped forward toward the obvious leader of the guardsmen.

"My good gentleman, we are overjoyed to see the envoys of the emir. I was hoping he would send reinforcements to aid us in our time of need."

The leader stopped, his mouth hanging open as the words he'd intended to say conflicted with Sinbad's welcome. Before he had a chance to start again. Sinbad moved quickly and seized his hand and shook it vigorously.

"Ah, *effendi*, truly it is a blessing from Allah that you have shown up at such a fortuitous time. Why we were just going back to our camp to gather more workers to help remove the fabulous treasure we discovered here, but," Sinbad paused and waved a hand to encompass everyone standing in front of him, "with your appearance, there should be no issues at all retrieving all the gold and gems we've discovered. But you must move quickly."

"And why is that?" the guard asked, squinting his eyes at Sinbad.

Ignoring the suspicious tone in the guard's voice, Sinbad continued, "Why, you've heard this is a magical city. Well, the treasury can only be reached before the moon has risen. I swear to you, it is a veritable mountain of wealth. Why, I'd wager one could set themselves up as an emir in their own right and still have enough to shower upon your master."

The guard's greed and loyalty were wavering, so Sinbad pushed a bit harder. "*Effendi*, to show you I speak the truth, I place myself and my men in your care.

We shall wait just outside the city with whatever retinue you wish to guard us with. If you return without the treasure, by all means, you can have our heads, and we shall not resist."

Henri picked up on Sinbad's cue and called out in a sad voice. "Captain, that's not fair. It's just a few blocks away in the building with the pointed arches. You can't just let them have it. We worked hard for that treasure. Why are you just giving it away?"

"Henri, it's only right. Besides, dead men can't spend treasure. I'm certain once these men see how much treasure there is, why they wouldn't even deny us a morsel or two."

The guard wanted to call Sinbad's bluff, but before he could speak again, one of the other guardsmen spoke up. "A few blocks away?"

Henri nodded vigorously. "Just go down this street until you see the fountain and turn to the right. There's no way to miss the treasury."

That was all it took. The guards hustled Sinbad's crew out of the city and assigned a few guards to watch them while the others, almost dragging their leader with them, rushed off, visions of mountains of gold and gems driving them forward. Sinbad and the rest of his crew plopped down on the ground and began talking among themselves. As they waited, Sinbad noticed their guards were eyeing the gate anxiously.

Ralf poked William and pointed toward the gate. "You know, if men like this are the norm, I'm glad I came to the desert lands. The trust they hold for one another is beyond anything I've ever seen in my travels. It's impressive the way they're faithfully guarding us while their friends fill their sacks with the finest gems and jewelry I'd ever seen. I'm certain their friends will share evenly with these guys."

William nodded. "I agree. It's fantastic to see such trust among guardsmen. Why, in my lands, it's for certain if I'd been left guarding some prisoners, my old companions would have exited the other direction with all the gold, leaving me holding the bag. It's so good to be in a land where everyone's companions are so trustworthy."

Seeing the guards eyeing the gate cautiously, Ralf continued. "You're right, my friend. And can you believe the steadfast loyalty this emir command? I mean, I'm certain the emir will share that immense wealth with them instead of simply keeping it all for himself."

Before Ralf had finished speaking, the remaining guards deserted their positions and rushed into the city to line their pockets with the treasures within. Only a few minutes after the last guard had disappeared, the sun hit the edge of the horizon, and the city began to shimmer. As the sun's ray disappeared, so did the city, becoming translucent, then transparent, and finally disappearing as completely as the morning mist burns off the sea, leaving behind only the depression in the center of the bluff to show it was ever there.

"That was a dirty trick, Sinbad," Adara said, staring at the nothingness that Umar had left behind.

"I think it was a rather dirty trick for the emir to send those men after us. I mean, we could have possibly fought our way out of the city, but those archers forced my hand. I can only hope that Haroun made his way out without running into them."

Henri picked up a nearby rock and launched it into the middle of the depression. "What do we have to show for this expedition, Captain? If not for this young woman outfitting the trip, we'd be much worse off than we were when we started."

"Henri, do you always see the worst in things. Why we've had an adventure so immense, the world would never believe a word of it. Plus, we saved this young lady from a lifetime of servitude to an evil master," he pointed at Tara. "No, we didn't secure enough treasure to retire, but then again, who wants to retire? As long as Allah sends the wind to fill the *Blue Nymph*'s sails, there are voyages for us to go on."

There was a sudden movement from the direction of their camp and Sinbad saw Haroun making his way over to join the crew. "Ah, praise Allah, you are safe. I was unable to warn you of the ambush waiting for you due to the small matter of being tied up. It took me quite a while to get myself free. I swear, some of those guards must have been sailors in another life."

Sinbad rushed forward and clasped his lookout on the shoulder. "Haroun, you're safe. We'd about given up hope on you when we couldn't find you in the city."

The curly-haired young man clapped Sinbad back on the shoulder in relief. "Captain, I felt the same. I don't know what happened, but after yesterday, I couldn't find anyone in the city besides myself and the crewmen with me. We searched most of the day but there was no sign of you anywhere."

"We'll fill you in when we get back to camp. So, when did these guardsmen appear?"

"We had just finished our last trip out of the city and were setting up for dinner when they appeared. Apparently, they captured our lookouts before they could raise the alarm and then fell on the camp. I ordered the men to surrender, as woefully outnumbered as we were. They secured all of us and then moved to the city to set an ambush for you. I don't see any of them and you are here, so I'm guessing they didn't find you?"

"No, they had us dead to rights, but thank Allah, their greed was larger than their sense of duty. I convinced them I had found a great treasure in the city, and they decided to seize it for themselves. Now, they will be trapped in the city for the rest of their lives."

"And this treasure?"

Sinbad laughed. "We found no treasure. We're as poor as the day we set out on this trip."

Haroun's eyes lit up and he shook his head. "Oh, no, Captain. For once, Haroun knows more than you do."

"Oh? Well then spit it out, you monkey."

Haroun motioned for the crew to follow him. Irritated but curious, Sinbad followed after his crewman and he and the rest of the crew made their way to the camp. They set to freeing the rest of his crew while Haroun took a position over next to their supply tent. Eventually, everyone gathered near the flap of the tent and Haroun flipped the tent open with a flourish, revealing barrels and boxes of supplies.

Ralf let out a derisive bark of a laugh. "Yes, now I see why Omar calls you Monkey. We've all seen supplies before."

Haroun's smile grew even broader. "Ah, but oh master of words, have you ever seen supplies like these?"

With that, he tipped one of the boxes over and the lid came off revealing a chest stuffed with gold coins. With a rush, the rest of the crew who'd been with Sinbad moved into the supply tent, opening barrels filled with gems and boxes filled with the finest of jewelry and statuary just below a thin covering of traveling equipment and supplies.

"But, how? When?" Ralf stuttered as he ran his hands through the gold coins.

"As I said, I had been searching for you for quite some time when I found a locked building." He flexed his fingers and continued. "Well, a locked-for-the-moment building. Apparently, we found the city's main treasury. We've spent all day today making trip after trip to load up what we could on our camels and bring it back here. We carefully placed all the remaining supplies on top and, thank Allah we had that foresight."

He made a rude gesture toward where the city had been before continuing. "We'd just made our last trip and secured everything when those guardsmen fell on us. I took them around and showed them these boxes, but they were not curious enough to dig through them once they saw what lay atop. I told them I was a mere sailor, and my captain was seeking the treasure within the city. I laid it on thick about what we hoped to find. Perhaps with my story and yours, Captain, we gave them just enough bait and they bit on the hook."

"Hmm, I will have to keep an eye on you from now on, Haroun, or soon you'll be master of the *Blue Nymph* and I'll be standing in the rigging watching the horizon."

"You have nothing to fear, Captain. Our talk about becoming the Emir of the Sea aside, I like being a lookout. I get tired just watching how much work you put in before each voyage. No, let those like Omar or William dream of command someday. I'm quite comfortable in my rigging."

"Well said, Haroun. Wait, did I hear something about dinner being prepared? Unless those raiders ate our food before coming after us."

"No worries, Captain. One evening meal coming up."

The smell of a sea breeze told Sinbad they were near the coast and as the camels made their way over a large ridge, the sight of the *Blue Nymph* safely anchored in the bay below brightened Sinbad's mood. The camels apparently took note of the captain's excitement and began picking up speed as they made their way down the ridge toward the sparkling blue water at the end of the trail.

Omar led the skeleton crew in a mad rush to meet the oncoming caravan and Sinbad slid off his camel to meet his first mate half-way. "You old sea dog. Praise Allah, it is good to see you."

"And you too, Sinbad. I'm even happy to see Monkey there. And from the expression on his face, I have a feeling I'm going to be hearing all about this excursion for the next few months in varying degrees of excruciating detail."

"Do not be too hard on the young man, Omar. Without his quick wits, we'd certainly be meeting you with a much dourer look than we do today. He had made the crew proud this trip."

"Monkey?" He glanced up at the heavens. "Of course, Allah would ensure I was stuck on the boat and miss seeing this miracle for myself."

Sinbad could only shake his head and fell to quickly organizing the crew to load the remaining supplies and the treasure onto the boat. It took several hours to get ready, and Sinbad decided they'd spend one last night ashore before setting sail to Basrah. The crew quickly dug a shallow pit and filled it with charcoal to fix the night's feast and as the stars began appearing in the night sky, the crew mingled as the shore crew regaled those who'd stayed behind with the ship with tales of their trek through the desert.

The moon was high overhead when the noise of the feast began to settle, and Sinbad snagged the last two kufta off of the spit and walked back into the shadows of small tree. He'd just leaned back, staring at his ship bobbing in the gentle waves washing ashore when he realized he wasn't alone.

"So, what now, Sinbad? The stories were true. You have more than enough treasure from this trip to retire peacefully anywhere you'd like."

"Adara, I spoke truly our last day at the city, I have no intentions to retire.

There are too many other ports I haven't been to yet. After splitting up the profits with the crew and reoutfitting the ship, I will use much of the money to help the poor in Basrah, Estafan, and other port cities. Besides, I think there's a gentleman waiting for me back in Basrah I once did some wrong to. Perhaps, with a small stipend, he can re-establish his good name and fortunes."

He leaned back against the tree, tucking his arms behind his head, staring out over the ocean. "No, I am a sailor, and my place is on the waters. I like coming ashore every so often, but there is no way I could ever leave the sea permanently. As long as there is a horizon out there I haven't seen the other side of, there'll always be something calling to me."

"And what will you do with me?"

"With you?"

The ifritah sat down beside him with her eyes downcast. Sinbad could see the nervousness in her demeanor and her voice was soft as she spoke again. "I betrayed you. I deliberately led you into the jann's clutches and was hoping you'd meet a horrible end. I know now that my anger was misplaced and that you are a good man. Still, I have conspired against you and willingly submit myself to your judgement."

"Who am I to judge you? Allah knows how many times I have acted in haste and anger in my life. I am the last person to hold your actions against you after you proved yourself against Zophar. It could not have been easy to overcome his influence, yet, if you had not released us, we'd have been trapped in that forbidden city for eternity."

He turned and smiled at her. "Besides, there are too few truly beautiful women in the world. Why would I deprive it of one such as yourself? The children of fire couldn't have chosen a better ambassador to represent themselves to the children of man if they had intentionally planned our meeting."

Adara blushed and Sinbad saw wisps of fire coming from the tips of her ears. "I have been warned about your flattering tongue, Sinbad."

"Oh? Do tell," Sinbad said, leaning toward the ifritah . . .

There was a pause as the storyteller took a drink from a nearby cup and the crowd pressed in closer. "What next, Malik? You can't end the story there."

"My dear friends, it would be rude not to close the door there. After all, if you want to hear more about the mighty Sinbad and what adventures the ifritah and peri may have had with his heroic crew, well, as they say, 'all will be revealed in the next chapter.'"

The crowd muttered about stopping just as it got to the good part, but the coins flew through the air and soon the blanket in front of Malik was covered in a veritable carpet of gold and silver. Finally, only a few children still hung around and Malik chased them off with some good-natured warnings. Gathering his items, he picked up his walking stick and shuffled off into the darkness.

A voice called out to him, and he stopped, a smile of recognition crossing his face as a familiar shadow stepped out from behind a tent. "All will be revealed in the next chapter?"

Malik moved closer, keeping his voice low. "Of course. Never tell the entire story in one setting. Always leave them wanting more and you'll have an even bigger audience the next time."

The shadowy figure nodded. "I see you're enjoying your time with this caravan."

"I am. It is a much different experience than the last time the two of us traveled together. We are not driven by any deadline other than how far our camels can go in one sitting." Malik glanced around and when they were certain no one could observe them, there was a shimmering aura around them and a beautiful ifritah was revealed. She rushed over to the shadowy figure and threw her arms around him.

"It has been too long, Sinbad."

"It has. I heard your caravan was coming this direction and came out to meet you. I didn't think you would mind."

"Mind, you idiot? I'm overjoyed. But are you staying with the caravan until it reaches Baghdad or will you be moving on again?"

"That, Adara, will be revealed in the next chapter."

THE END

An Opportunity Presents Itself

I first discovered the wonders of Shahrazad when I was still in elementary school. My aunt had a set of the *The Reader's Digest Best Loved Books* and along with discovering *The Jungle Book, Robin Hood,* and so on, *The Thousand and One Arabian Nights* caught my fascination, but of all the stories, I really fell in love with Sinbad and Ali Baba. Several years later, I caught the spectacle of the Ray Harryhausen versions of Jason and Sinbad, especially *Sinbad and the Eye of the Tiger.* Those movies were absolutely fascinating to watch, and as I attended college and took some film classes, I could easily appreciate the mastery that had gone into those stop-motion scenes. What I also appreciated is the action never got in the way of the story, which is something I've tried to apply to my writing.

So, when I got the chance to pitch something to Airship 27, and saw that Sinbad was available, I had to jump at the opportunity. I dove into the research and unfortunately, my Arabic skills are not good enough to *Alf-layla wa layla*, I grabbed my copy of Richard Burton's translation of Shahrazad's beautiful tale and re-read all the Sinbad stories just to get a good feel for the originals. While I knew Airship 27's stories were unique unto themselves, I wanted to be as true to the spirit of the Sinbad stories as I could be. But, what to write about?

I decided to put my old skills as a history major to use and dove into Arabic mythology and folktales. I found a reference to the "Atlantis of the Sands" and discovered several legends about lost cities in the Arabian desert that had disappeared usually to due to Allah's punishment or some supernatural causes. When I saw the legend of Ubar had been misattributed to T.H. Lawrence and also *Alf layla wa layla*, I knew I had my setting. Then it was just a matter of doing a little research on Arabic seafaring in the that time period, reading some of the other Sinbad stories that had already been released by Airship 27 and voila, the story outline fell into place.

I had a ball writing this story and hope to return to our intrepid band of "merchants" sometime in the future. I just hope you enjoyed this story as much as I did writing it. *Ma'a salaam, effendi.*

RICHARD C. WHITE - is a science fiction/fantasy/fantasy noir/action-adventure/non-fiction author. His latest release, *On Wings of Steel,* a steampunk novel, was released in April 2025. Other works include *Chasing Danger: The Case Files of Theron Chase, Harbinger of Darkness, For a Few Gold Pieces More,* and *Terra Incognito,* a non-fiction book on world building. He's appeared in the Origins Game Fair anthologies (*Monsters, Robots,* and *Space),* as well as in pulp anthologies such as *Thrilling Adventure Yarns 2021, Liberty Girl: Fight for Freedom, All for One: Tales of the Musketeers, The New Adventures of Rocky Jordan* and *Charles Boeckman Presents: Johnny Nickle.* Rich has other works scheduled for release in 2025 and early 2026 with more to come.

As a media tie-in writer, he's written for *Star Trek, Doctor Who, Battletech,* and *The Incredible Hulk* franchises. His novel, *Gauntlet Dark Legacy: Paths of Evil,* was a best-selling tie-in for his publisher. His latest tie-in works are *One Night in Freeport* and *Storm Wreck* for Nisaba Press (Green Ronin Gaming).

Richard is a member of the Science Fiction and Fantasy Writers of America and the International Association of Media Tie-in Writers. Additionally, Richard serves on the SFWA Writer Beware committee.

THE DEVIL AHEAD, THE DEVIL BEHIND

by Fred Adams, Jr.

The gentle afternoon breeze set the curtains swaying and brought the scent of Kartesh's harbor to mingle with the perfume of the lavish bedchamber. Sinbad lay between silken sheets, hands behind his head. The fair-skinned woman lay curled against him, her pale arm a contrast to his mocha-colored chest. Her golden hair fanned out over his shoulder.

"Sing me a song, Sinbad."

The Captain laughed. "I am not much for singing, Katrina. My voice in song would drive you from me."

"A poem then—something romantic. I want words."

"Then words you shall have." Sinbad frowned, thinking then smiled and said:

Your lips are the hue of amethyst,
Your hair like strands of gold,
Your eyes, they glow as sapphires,
All make a man so bold,
To reach for such forbidden fruit,
And hold it in my hand,
Fills my heart with gladness . . .

Sinbad hesitated.

"Yes? Yes? Finish the poem."

"Please, let me think. Ah."

Fills my heart with gladness that,
You are woman; I am man.

Katrina laughed with delight and nuzzled his throat. "Do you love me, Sinbad?"

"As I love all women, Katrina," he replied. "After my ship and the sea and adventure."

"Not even third place?" She pouted. "Take me away from here, Sinbad. Mustapha disgusts me. To him I am no more than another possession. Why my father ever brought me from the North to arrange my marriage to that fat, sweaty pig, I will never understand."

"It could be that his proffer of dowry outshone all others."

"Like a slave at an auction," she grumbled.

"Like a rare jewel, such as none has seen before, my beauty." He paused. "Hearth and home are not for me, my love. You would soon tire of life at sea, Katrina, and on land you would likewise quickly tire of my absence. Besides, you have grown accustomed to luxury and ease that my ship cannot provide. Let us enjoy today and not care for the morrow."

Her pout disappeared at the suggestion. Katrina's eyes sparkled. "Yes, let us enjoy today—again. We—"

A knock at the door. "Mistress." An urgent female voice. "The Master has returned."

"Curse him," Katrina hissed. "Mustapha was to be gone til tomorrow."

"Time I bid farewell."

Sinbad threw back the sheets, bundled his clothes and shoes and without hesitation threw them through the open window to the garden below. He turned back to kiss Katrina one last time then leapt naked from the casement, wrapping his arms around the trunk of a tall palm that grew just outside the window. He shinned down the tree, hearing the shouts of two voices from the bedchamber, pulled on his pantaloons, and vaulted the low garden wall. Once in the street, he put his feet into his shoes and pointed them toward the harbor and his ship.

The Blue Nymph lay moored in Kartesh's busy harbor among a variety of vessels; galleys, dhows, Gaouls, biremes, and barges, ships from every land. But none compared to the sleek beauty of the Blue Nymph, a perfect blend of maneuverability, durability, and speed. Where other ships plowed the waves, the Blue Nymph seemed to glide over them, buoyed by the hand of Mother Ocean who tolerated the passage of other ships across her face but indulged the Blue Nymph as if she were her favorite child.

Sinbad, unless he were running for his life, always stopped for a moment when he caught sight of his beloved ship to appreciate her graceful lines, crafted as if a deity were her chandler, and to thank the Fates who delivered her to him.

The Blue Nymph resembled the Phoenician vessels that sailed around the Earth to trade and barter, but her lines were styled at unique angles; a sharper prow, a narrower hull, and a higher stern that gave her the appearance that she were speeding over the waves even when bobbing at anchor. Her blue sails were furled now as she lay at rest for her next journey.

Sinbad approached her from her stern, and as was his custom, blew a kiss to the mermaid elaborately carved there. Legend had it that the demigod Theseus shaved the hair from the front half of his head only because he would never turn his back to flee an enemy who might seize it from behind. Sinbad reasoned that instead of a figurehead on her prow that a rival or enemy might see on her approach, another ship would soon see only her stern as she pulled away from it at speed.

The mermaid was robust, full-bosomed, her lovely face full of mischief. Her scaly tail curled like a hand, inviting pursuit and mocking its futility in the same gesture. Her every aspect said, "Catch me if you can." One of the sapphire blue globes of her eyes caught the late sun and seemed to wink at Sinbad in return for his gesture.

Most of his crew of two dozen were ashore enjoying their last day in port before setting sail again. Only a few drew the lot to remain on board to guard the Blue Nymph from intruders. Two of them flanked the gang plank, one of them, Jafari, the tall, lean Watusi tribesman, enslaved by Arab invaders as a boy and apprenticed to the sea. His skill with a harpoon was unsurpassed. Fathi, the short, muscular Copt whose name meant "victory" stood beside him. Both looked to be at their ease, but Sinbad knew that at the first sign of trouble, the pair would be blades out and deadly.

"*Tahiaati, Kabtin,*" the Copt said, a slight nod of his head acknowledging Sinbad's station.

"Was your time ashore productive, Captain?" Jafari's deep voice rumbled. He gave a sly smile that showed his golden teeth and slid his short sword back and forth halfway in and out of its sheath. "I hope not *re*-productive."

Sinbad laughed at the jest. "I am never certain, Jafari. I am always an ocean away before the fact could be known. Someday, perhaps, I will see my face on some youth and he see his on me, and both will wonder which of us is the mirror."

All laughed at that, and Sinbad climbed aboard his ship. He called back to the sentries, "I am here now to watch her; go enjoy a last drink or two. There are no ten brigands that Omar and I cannot handle. Just be back by half-night." He tossed a coin to each of them.

"Many thanks, Captain," Fathi said, and Jafari echoed the Copt's gratitude. Sinbad boarded the Blue Nymph, and gone was the sensation of rigid earth below his feet. The deck below him rose and fell like the breast of a sleeping lover. He was home.

Omar, his first mate and long-time navigator, sat on a keg on the deck staring out at the ocean, elbow on his knee and chin on his fist. The sunset dyed his thick grey beard a russet hue and deepened the furrows of his forehead.

"Omar, why are you here? You should go ashore for a night of pleasure before we sail."

"Too often, Sinbad, when I do, I end up with another wife. I have had six already and a dozen children. And if I go ashore, I will likely drink myself blind. Who will steer the ship at dawn after the crew carries me aboard? Better I stay where I am."

Sinbad watched the sun slowly sink over the harbor, feeling its rays warm his face. His sinewy forearms lay crossed on the taffrail as the Blue Nymph rose and fell gently with the evening tide. In a few hours the crew would return, their shore leave over.

"Red sky at night," said Omar, leaning at the rail beside him. "Should be good sailing on the morrow."

"Kartesh has been kind to us, but sooner or later, we wear out our welcome in any port. Besides, I feel an itch to be at sea again."

"As do I." Omar ran his fingers through his beard. "I have sailed Mother Ocean for so many years that solid ground under my feet seems almost unnatural."

"I understand your sentiment, old friend, but it is hard to deny the pleasures of the harbor."

Samson, the Blue Nymph's mascot and mouser rubbed against Sinbad's calf. The big grey Persian cat earned his keep by killing the ever-present rats that crept on board at every landfall to gorge themselves on the ship's larder and leave their stool behind as an insult.

Sinbad reached down and ruffled the cat's scruffy fur, and Samson purred in contentment. He enjoyed the attention for a moment, then in a breath, the mouser's body stiffened. Samson's whiskers twitched, and his body lowered. He slunk away from Sinbad, in a sinuous crouch, eyes fixed on a coil of rope a few steps away.

"Looks as if Samson may have found his supper," Sinbad said with a laugh.

"I believe Allah created food to sustain and satisfy Man, and *Shaitan* created rats to even the score."

"And cats maintain the balance."

Samson seemed to flow like quicksilver across the deck toward the coil of hemp, one paw ahead of the other. His chin brushed the teak as he crept toward his prey. The rat sprang from the coil and scuttled across the deck. It darted from one corner to another with Samson in pursuit. It was quick, but Samson was quicker.

The cat cornered its prey between a water cask and a bulkhead. The rat was a big one, but instead of baring its teeth and bracing to defend itself, it seemed to cower, fearful, into the nook. Samson batted at the creature with his paw.

Sinbad and Omar watched as Nature's drama played out toward its inevitable denouement.

"I have always wondered why cats toy with their prey before they eat it,"

Sinbad said. "Impending doom seems more cruel to endure than the death blow."

"When have you ever known Nature to be kind?" Omar replied. "The weak feed the strong. Perhaps the terror makes the meat taste sweeter," Omar stood. "I will leave Samson to enjoy his meal. I have much to prepare for the morrow." He walked away, leaving Sinbad at the rail. The Captain turned back to the sunset when he heard a raspy, high-pitched voice.

"Sinbad! Sinbad! Save me!"

He turned and looked around him but saw no one on the deck.

Again the voice. "Help, Sinbad! Help!" It came from the corner of the deck where Samson held his prey at bay. Every time the rat would move one way or the other, Samson would bat it with a paw and knock it back into the corner. Once more, Sinbad heard the voice. "Save me! Save me, I beg you!"

Sinbad's hand shot out and he grabbed the tom cat's scruff, holding him back, but ready to loose him again should the rat try to run.

"Please!" the rat squeaked. "Save me from that monster!"

Sinbad had sailed all seven of the seas and seen many strange lands. He had encountered talking beasts before, but had never seen nor heard of a talking rat. The proverbial fate of cats notwithstanding, he gave in to curiosity.

"I will save you my rodent friend—for now, but if you try to run away, I will send Samson after you and this time not interrupt his kill."

"I will not flee, Sinbad. I swear it."

Sinbad dropped Samson into an empty barrel over the cat's protest. As quick as Samson, Sinbad seized the rat behind its head and pushed it into a fish trap lying on the deck nearby, effectively caging it. Instead of alarm at confinement, the rat seemed almost relieved. Sinbad held the cage even with his face; the creature's dark fur was matted, raw patches of flesh showing from recent battles won or lost. The captain looked the rat in its eyes, eyes which instead of tiny beads of ebony or ruby, glowed green with white ringing the iris—the slanting eyes of a human.

"I see the hand of sorcery here. Why are you on the Blue Nymph, rat? Were you sent to spy on me? Or are you come to curse my ship?"

"No, no, esteemed Captain," the rat said, peering through the woven mesh of the trap. "I come to beg your help. What I say is for your ears alone. May we go to a place where we might speak unheard?"

The deck was empty, but Sinbad took the trap and the rat to his cabin, first tipping the barrel and freeing Samson. The cat hissed and glared at the rat, then hissed and glared at his master for denying his meal. Sinbad took a dried fish from a nearby urn and threw it to Samson, who set upon it with voracious appetite.

"That, friend rat, shall be your fate should I find you deceitful."

To that, the caged rodent shuddered but made no reply.

Sinbad took the trap to his cabin and set it on the table. He struck flint to steel and lit the oil lamp that hung from a gimbal on the wall, throwing the room into a brassy glow.

"Now, rodent, your story—in detail."

"Captain Sinbad, you said you see the hand of sorcery. I am its victim. My name is Plazzo." The rat pronounced the name "Plat-zo" as the people of the island of Sicily in the Mediterranean might. "I am apprenticed to the sorcerer Vatlek. My master, angry with me, put me in this form and threw me out in the street to fend for myself. I have survived three days and nights, skulking from one alley to another, battling other rats for scraps of cast-off food, and scampering for my life. There are more damnable cats in Kartesh than hairs on your head—before you shaved it, that is."

Sinbad laughed in spite of himself, running a palm over his slick scalp. "But what brought you here, Plazzo?"

"Hiding in a nook in a tavern, I overheard men talking about the great Captain Sinbad, renowned as a fearless adventurer and a man of great cunning, and frankly, no offense to you, the most skilled thief on the continent. Only you can help me."

"How might I do that? I am no wizard. If you are a sorcerer's apprentice, you surely know magic. Why not simply cast another spell and make yourself human again?"

"I have learned much from Vatlek," Plazzo said, "but not enough to undo what he has done. I do not know the words that can restore me to my rightful form."

"What did you do to anger your master so?"

"When a man fills his mind with knowledge of so narrow a subject, it often crowds out other things, like pouring water into a bowl already filled. What was there before spills out over the rim. Vatlek's obsession with the dark arts has crowded out his patience, his compassion, his humanity. I erred in mixing a potion, and he flew into a rage. He spoke his words, I fell down in a swound, and when I woke, I had paws instead of hands and feet, and whiskers. Vatlek towered over me like a giant. He cast me into the street, and for three days I have survived more by chance than by skill."

"I still do not understand how I might help you."

"With your skills and daring, you can return me to the sorcerer's palace, I can lead you to his inner chamber where his grimoire—"

"Grimoire? I know not that word."

"—his book of spells is kept, and if you can open it for me, I can find the words to restore myself."

"Steal from a sorcerer? You must be mad, Plazzo. He would turn me into a rat like yourself, or worse. Even if I could get into his palace and find this book, surely it is guarded by things living and not."

"I am not without power myself. I can ensure your safety. Yes, there are traps, but I know where they are. There are Guardians that protect Vatlek's palace, but I have served the wizard for decades, and have a good memory. The right words from me, and the Guardians will be as docile as lambs. I do not want you to steal the book, simply open it and turn its pages until I find the spell that will restore me."

"And then?"

"I will recite it and return myself to human form."

"And why should I help you?"

The rat made a choking, gagging noise and its body rippled. It coughed up a golden ring with an emerald as big as the tip of Sinbad's thumb that clattered on the table top and glowed in the lamplight. "There is much more to come for you. Remember, Sinbad, I too am a sorcerer, not so powerful as he, but I can reward you in more ways than gold if you help to restore me."

Sinbad held the ring between his thumb and forefinger. He poured red wine from a decanter on the table over it to wash away the rat's bile and studied it in the glow of the lamp. Never had he seen such a gem as that set in the ring. Its weight, its cut, its clarity told him that a handful of these could buy him a new ship, a palace, or almost a kingdom. "And there is more of this?"

"Gold, and rubies, and pearls, and diamonds—a caliph's ransom—all you can carry if only you will help me."

"And why should I trust your word, Plazzo?"

"Trust your own eyes instead. I am a rat, but a rat that still knows magic. The rat squeaked words in a guttural language that Sinbad did not recognize. The ship's cabin shimmered around him, and faded into a grey twilight, replaced by a room heaped with treasure of every description. Flickering light from the lamps danced on the facets of gems and the faces of coins. "Vatlek's treasure vault," Plazzo said.

Sinbad looked around him in wonder. The room held more wealth than a kingdom's treasury. "If you could enjoy such wealth and what it can purchase, why did you not cease with magic and live to a comfortable old age?"

"The treasure is not mine; it is Vatlek's, although I could have taken as much of it as I wished and lived well to my end. I do not give up magic for the same reason that you do not give up the sea and adventure. You have won many a fortune in your travels, Sinbad, then gambled and caroused it away, but wealth is not your joy. We are, both of us, men of passion, you for adventure, I for the power that the dark arts give me. Such passions are glowing coals in your heart and mine that only death can extinguish. Wealth is no more to you, nor to me, nor to Vatlek than a tool, a means to pursue what we really desire."

Sinbad reached out to thrust his hand into a chest of golden coins, and his hand thumped on the table. In an instant, the treasure room was gone.

"Now you have seen what awaits if you help me. Take that ring as my gift. It is a protection. While you wear it, neither sword nor spear will pierce you, no storm winds will rend your sails, no lightning will strike your mast. If you have the spine for my quest, put it on your left hand, nearer your heart, and let us get on with it. I weary of scuttling about on four feet and eating offal."

Sinbad sat for a long moment, chin in his hand, pondering Plazzo's words. Putting himself between two wizards was at best a risky proposition, but the longer he gazed at the shining gem in his palm, the less he feared the risk. The rat watched the Captain as he stared at the ring for a moment longer then thrust it onto his finger. It seemed a little large at first but shrunk to fit perfectly below his second knuckle. He felt a wave of dizziness for a few seconds, replaced with a sense of might and confidence.

"Tell me more about this palace."

The streets of Kartesh were never empty. Like the dusky transition between sunset and nightfall, as the day folk ended their business, closed their shops, and went to their homes, the night people emerged. Taverns and brothels came alive with revelers. Vendors of every vice took over the streets, and their customers were legion. Anything not sold by the daylight merchants was proffered openly from dark doorways. Likewise, brigands of every stripe prowled Kartesh's byways, from cut purse to assassin, but Sinbad strode those streets unafraid. One look at his well-muscled body and the scimitar that hung between his shoulder blades was sufficient to warn away most miscreants. Add a rat perched on his shoulder like a favored pet, and the night people stared as he passed, but none dared approach him.

Not all men are sensible, however. Away from the bustle of the bazaar, Plazzo directed Sinbad down a shadowy street. Too far down to retreat, Plazzo sniffed and his whiskers twitched. "I smell trouble." Two ruffians stepped into Sinbad's path, and he smelled them too, a mix of unwashed bodies, garlic, and wine.

"What have we here?" The taller of the brigands, a dark-bearded brute in a striped caftan said. "A rat and a rat." He reached into his garments and his fist came out wrapped around the haft of a hammer, as a butcher in a slaughterhouse might use to stun a steer before cutting its throat.

"And one of them a blackamoor rat." The Brute's shorter companion wore little more than rags. His clothing was tattered, but the wicked poniard he held by its handle was of the finest quality. "I like that embroidered vest, Malo. I think it would hang well on my shoulders, eh?" Then to Sinbad, "Take it off."

Sinbad did not move. He heard stealthy steps behind him. Plazzo shifted on his shoulder.

"I said take it off, Moor." Rags laughed. "I do not want it soiled with your blood."

Malo took a step forward and raised his hammer. "And I will take that ring. Give it to me."

"Now," Plazzo hissed and sprang from Sinbad's shoulder to sink his teeth into the throat of the robber who crept up behind them. The thief dropped his dagger and shrieked, batting at the rat that clung by its jaws to his neck.

Sinbad reached behind for his scimitar, dodging a blow from Malo's hammer that would have smashed his skull. He brought the sword around in a deadly arc that cleanly sliced through the brute's wrist. The hand and hammer fell to the cobblestones. Malo screamed, staring at the stump of his arm as it pumped his life away.

That left Rags, who, seizing the opportunity, stepped in and thrust his poniard at Sinbad's chest. Instead of piercing the Captain's heart, the tip stopped at his skin. Sinbad's blade flashed, and the puzzled look on Rags' face remained as his head fell to the pavement and rolled into the gutter. His headless corpse teetered for a moment as if deciding which way to fall then pitched over onto the street.

The third robber lay bleeding out as Plazzo tore goblets of flesh from his throat and gulped them down. He looked up at Sinbad and said, "Do not stare at me so. I have not eaten today."

Sinbad scooped up the rat and set him once again on his shoulder. "Time to move on before the City Watch finds us here with three dead men."

"Now you know I spoke truth," Plazzo said. "The ring protected you."

To that, Sinbad could make no argument.

At Plazzo's direction, Sinbad carried him through the lamplit avenues and alleys, past the homes of the respectable and into the neighborhood of the rich, whose great houses hid behind high walls and iron gates, lives contained and secure from the perils outside.

"Here." Plazzo said.

Sheer walls three fathoms tall surrounded an unseen edifice and hid it from view.

"I see no gate, Plazzo" Sinbad said. "And this wall offers no purchase to scale it."

"None that you can see."

"Then how—"

"Follow the wall around the corner."

"And you are certain that Vatlek is away?"

"If he were here, I would sense his presence, just as he would sense my own."

Around the corner, Sinbad saw an unbroken continuation of the wall. "Go to the center," the rat commanded.

Plazzo spoke words Sinbad had never heard, and a section of the wall shimmered like ripples in a pond, and he saw a two-leaved gate twice his height. Its iron bars were twisted into strange shapes and symbols.

"Your entrance," the rat said. "Another word, and the gates swung inward on silent hinges.

Sinbad stared at the top of the portal and wondered what creatures existed that so tall a gateway was built to accommodate them. He drew a long breath and passed through it into a flagstone courtyard ringed with tall bushes. He looked behind him and saw the gate shimmer and merge once again into a featureless wall. It is a trick, he thought, an illusion like the vision of the treasure vault, or is it? Sinbad reached out a hand and felt the smooth, featureless wall where the gate had been.

"Do not worry," Plazzo said. "When the time comes to depart, it will become a portal again."

The courtyard opened at one hand onto a formal garden of fragrant night-blooming flowers and graceful palms around a fountain whose waters glittered in the moonlight; on the other, a patch of stunted trees, twisted bushes, and strange plants. The night breeze shifted and wafted a noxious odor that stung Sinbad's nostrils.

"The Master's *hadīqa*," Plazzo said, "where I tend the mandrakes, the belladonna, and the nightshade for his potions—those and others with no names. The flowers' scent counters the stench when the wind is right."

"On the one hand, Paradise; on the other, Perdition. A garden of Good and Evil."

The rat chittered in unexpected amusement. "Yes, I suppose it is. Move ahead." Past the courtyard, the palace rose into the night sky, impossibly tall to be unseen from the outside. Sinbad had to tilt his head backward to see the tops of its minarets. The architecture was elaborate; decorative cornices, oriels, balconies, latticed windows, and gold filigree everywhere. Sinbad had seen the palaces of kings, Sultans, and Caliphs, and few compared with the splendor he saw bathed in the moonlight.

A dark shape rose from the bushes with a menacing growl, a red-eyed shadow with no neck, whose face sprouted from its chest and arms reached

"A GARDEN OF GOOD AND EVIL"

the ground. Sinbad's scimitar flashed from its scabbard. Plazzo spoke a word, and the creature retreated in silence. "One of the Guardians," Plazzo said. "Let us go inside before more come."

The palace entrance was nearly as tall as the gates. The elaborately carved doors gave onto a cavernous anteroom so large that its dozen lamps on golden stands lit it dimly at best. The floor was a single slab of black marble, polished so brightly that Sinbad could look down from his full height and see himself as if he stood on a mirror. The face that looked back at him was creased with worry, its brow wrinkled and mouth set in a tight line. Missing was the brashness, the bravado, replaced not with fear but with wary caution. He felt a sense of vertigo staring into the blackness and had to tear his eyes away.

"Up those stairs," Plazzo said in his ear.

As the portals were tall, so the grand staircase was wide—wide enough to drive a carriage between its carved banisters. At its top, a corridor split to the left and to the right.

"Which way? Left or right?"

"Either way. The passage winds back on itself. Follow it entire, and you will find yourself where you began."

Good to know, thought Sinbad. Should Plazzo and I become separated I can find my way out of here. Sinbad had learned long before that luck favored his right hand, so that was the way he chose.

The corridor was narrower than the staircase and made odd angled turns. At intervals it gave onto open doorways where Sinbad saw spiral stairs winding upward into darkness, no doubt to the towers he had seen from the outside. Heavy curtains hung over windows at either hand. He pulled a drape aside, expecting a view of the palace grounds and saw instead the Kartesh marketplace. He thought at first it was a painting, then the people moved, walking, talking, plying their shady trades in the torchlight.

"What is this?" He asked. "We passed through the bazaar long ago."

"The Master's windows open onto many vistas," Plazzo said.

Sinbad parted the curtains on the next one and saw the Kartesh harbor, ships bobbing on the moonlit waves. A closer look showed him the mermaid stern of the blue nymph, safe at her mooring. A third window gave onto a landscape such as the Captain had never seen. The barren ground looked like a patch of warty skin rippling and folding upon itself. On its surface blue men, or what looked to be men scurried back and forth like ants from an overturned hill. As he watched in wonder, a creature with leathery wings swooped down from the yellow sky and seized of the blue figures in its talons and carried him away screaming. Sinbad drew the curtain.

"Vatlek's eyes," said Plazzo, matter-of-factly, "see many places. Keep moving."

Soon they came to an iron door with the face of a gorgon eye-to-eye cast in silver. From its mouth, a golden ring hung, a knocker. “Tap the door with the ring as I tell you. Three quick, two slow, two quick, three slow.”

Sinbad took the ring in his fingers, as he did, the gorgon’s face came alive. Its eyes blazed crimson, and the serpents on its head hissed and struck at his fingers. Sinbad let go of the ring and leapt backward, almost spilling Plazzo from his shoulder.

“Do not fear. She will not harm you. Show her the ring.”

Sinbad held the ring before the gorgon’s eyes, and their glow faded. The serpents settled once again.

“As I said, three quick, two slow, two quick, three slow.”

Sinbad did as Plazzo directed, and the door swung inward. Sinbad was about to cross the threshold when Plazzo said,

“Wait. Throw something ahead of you.”

“What should I throw?”

“Anything. Your shoe will suffice.”

Sinbad pulled a shoe from his foot and threw it through the doorway. A dozen razor-thin blades flashed from the top of the doorway to clang onto the stone threshold. The shoe was neatly severed in three pieces.

“Step over the blades with care. To touch an edge is to bleed.”

Once inside, Plazzo chirped three notes, and flames came alive in sconces, lighting the room. Sinbad recognized the treasure vault the rat showed him earlier, but this time, when he thrust his hand into a chest of golden coins, it came back full to overflowing.

“As promised, Sinbad. All you can carry, but first, the spell.”

Sinbad scooped a handful of gems from an urn and dropped them into a pocket of his pantaloons. If things went badly, he at least would be paid.

“To your left. The door.”

Beyond a heap of golden scepters, diadems, and tiaras Sinbad saw an alcove with an iron door. As he passed the pile of golden regalia, he wondered at the identity and the fate of so many rulers trading their crowns—for what? Victory over an enemy? Eternal youth? One’s love of a lifetime? He recalled with a shudder the words of an old Arab proverb: a gift from *Shaitan* is a debt in the end.

His hand closed on the door’s knob, and it writhed in his grip like something alive. He squeezed it more tightly and twisted it. The door swung inward, but Sinbad hesitated to step through it. “Must I sacrifice my other shoe?”

“There is no trap at this door. If one has gotten this far, he has earned the right to enter.”

“I’ll leave it open.” Sinbad’s years of adventure had taught him that it is the course of true wisdom to always leave a path of escape.

The chamber looked at first glance, octagonal, but on a more careful look, Sinbad counted nine black walls emblazoned with symbols and runes in gold. The room was lit by a lamp hung three-chained from the ceiling in the room's center. A glowing sphere rested in its bowl instead of an oil flame. When he looked overhead, Sinbad saw the starry expanse of the heavens painted in phosphorous on the black ceiling, but he saw no familiar constellations. Then a streak of light shot across the expanse, a shooting star, and he realized what he saw was no ceiling; it was the night sky—but what sky?

Standing still, he sensed a subtle movement in the walls. They seemed to gently expand then contract, as if the room were breathing, making the runes undulate.

An obsidian pedestal stood in the room's center, and on it, a book. "There," Plazzo said. "The grimoire."

The grimoire was bound in dark, scaly skin, its cover boards iron hinged. A clasp held it shut, but the lock devised by man did not exist that Sinbad could not pick. In a moment, the clasp sprang apart and swung away.

"Open it," Plazzo urged.

Sinbad hesitated, remembering the blades at the treasure vault door.

"There is no trap, fool. What kills you kills me as well," Plazzo said. "Open it!"

Sinbad took a breath, rubbed his palms together, leaned away from the pedestal and carefully took the cover by a corner and opened the book. No flechettes flew from the walls. No scorpions scuttled across the floor. The walls fluttered more quickly. The first page was emblazoned with a seven-pointed star, its lowest point projecting downward like the blade of a poniard and in its center, a staring eye. The eye seemed to look inside him, take his measure. Its enchantment was broken by Plazzo's squeak. "Turn the pages. I will tell you when to stop."

Each new page held another block of text penned in a spidery hand, or images so alien that Sinbad had to look away from them, lest they haunt his dreams forever: creatures with scores of eyes and tentacles like a kraken, or human torsos with the heads of fish, creatures furred and fanged, cities whose architecture conformed to impossible geometries twisted around themselves, charts of stars that in all his journeys, Sinbad had never seen in the night sky. He wanted to stop, to run out of the room, but felt compelled to continue, Plazzo peering intently from his shoulder.

He had turned more than a score of pages and was grateful when the rat said finally, "That page."

The parchment held a simple set of lines in Sanskrit, penned like a poem.

Sinbad began to read them aloud, sounding out unfamiliar words.

"Stop, you fool. Words said cannot be taken back. Who knows what an uninitiated voice like yours might loose on us."

"Then you say the spell," Sinbad said. "Free yourself, and let us leave this accursed place."

"That will not be necessary."

A new voice.

Sinbad turned and saw a crimson-robed figure in the doorway, a figure Sinbad knew must be Vatlek.

The sorcerer stood a head taller than Sinbad's six feet. He drew back the hood of his robe to reveal a face that at once looked youthful, yet whose eyes testified to more than one lifetime of wisdom.

The rat leapt from Sinbad's shoulder to the book, and then to the floor. "Please, Master! Restore me!" Plazzo implored.

"Very well." Vatlek's voice seemed to fill the room, and the walls danced wildly as he recited the incantation. Plazzo quivered and shook, and in a trice, stood beside Sinbad, once again a man.

Sinbad's first impression was that Plazzo perhaps looked better as a rat. What stood beside him was a balding naked man, his pink skin blotched and mottled. Plazzo sported an ample paunch and bony limbs. Wizened and all but toothless, the apprentice embodied old age. A pair of stubby horns poked through what thatch of grey hair remained on his scalp. Sinbad stared at Plazzo's toes, which, like his fingers, were webbed. He reached for his scimitar to pay Plazzo for his trickery, but found his arm would not obey him.

"Go and clothe yourself, Plazzo," the sorcerer said. "The sight of your nakedness offends my senses.

"Yes, Master." The apprentice genuflected and retreated through the doorway.

"Now, Sinbad, let us talk."

The sorcerer walked all around Sinbad, eyeing him from crown to soles, taking his measure. "You, unlike Plazzo, are a fine figure of a man, Captain. Praxiteles would have carved your likeness from a block of onyx. As you have doubtless discerned, I am Plazzo's master, Vatlek." He mouthed a word, and Sinbad felt his limbs loosen.

"Do not blame Plazzo for bringing you to me. His will is mine, as has been yours—from the moment you donned that ring."

Sinbad looked to his hand where the ring's emerald pulsed with a dull glow, a pulse that he felt with each heartbeat. He tugged at the ring to pull it off, but as he did, it squeezed tighter to the point of pain. When he let go, it relaxed again.

"And do not bother trying to cut off your finger, Captain. Plazzo spoke true. The ring is proof against harm to your body, even self-inflicted. You cannot escape my will even by suicide. Just as no man's blade can harm you, neither can your own. Only one thing can."

"And what is that?"

The sorcerer's laugh was mirthless. "I know. Plazzo knows, in case you stray from serving me. You will not know—that is, until it strikes you."

"Why am I here?" Sinbad asked.

"You are here because I need someone with your unique attributes. You are a master sea Captain, you have the swiftest ship on the ocean, you are also an accomplished thief, and you are the most daring among men. Only you, Sinbad, can undertake the task I require."

"And what task is that, Vatlek?"

"Something very valuable has been stolen from me. I need you to steal it back."

The sorcerer gestured, and the walls looked to dissolve into mist. As Vatlek told his tale, Sinbad saw the scenes as if actors performed a play around him.

"I am over a hundred-fifty years old."

Sinbad's expression revealed his skepticism.

"Believe it." Vatlek went on. "I was born the only child of Master Wizard Vashwal." Vatlek said the name with a mixture of reverence and resentment. "My mother, one of his concubines—Laea was her name—died in childbirth, and I grew up amid a world of sorcery. I was precocious; I learned quickly, and by young adulthood, I developed considerable skill.

"Lion sires sometimes eat their young because they fear the cub will grow strong as the sire grows weak with age and usurp his place in the pride. My father became wary of his scion. It seemed to him that I learned too much too quickly and would soon displace him, but I was too useful to be cast aside, so he did not destroy me. Instead, he kept me under his heel with the promise that soon—always soon—he would teach me the greatest secrets of his art.

"I saw the horrors that he inflicted upon his enemies. Should I have rebelled or tried to escape his iron will, my punishment would have been no less severe. I had no choice but to remain and serve.

"As you have doubtless guessed, the one secret even the great Vashwal did not possess was everlasting life. The day came when my father lay on his deathbed, and he still had not taught me his deepest secrets.

"I would not be cheated of my legacy. I had become powerful enough, and he had weakened enough that I imprisoned his *ruh*, his spirit as it left his mortal frame until a time when I could revive it and force him to reveal the promised secrets."

Before Sinbad's eyes, a jade statue appeared, floating in the air. It was roughly his own height, fashioned into a human form. Its visage was stern, menacing even. It glowered at him; a scowl of contempt mixed with frustration and rage.

"Your father?"

Vatlek nodded. "It is he."

"How long has he been imprisoned thus?"

"More years than your own as I have striven to learn and grow powerful enough to force his secrets from him."

"And this is what has been stolen."

"It is." Vatlek wrung his hands in frustration. "I was on the cusp of divining the means to bring him back, to force him to yield his power and magic to me when a rival sorcerer named Kabruk stole the statue from me, and with it my father's *ruh*. I must retrieve it, lest he do what I intended and with my father's powers, destroy me, along with his other rivals."

"Your palace is well-guarded. How did this Kabruk steal it?"

"He sent Philoctes, an adventurer like yourself under his protection who managed to enter my palace, my treasure vault, and this room unscathed. Philoctes escaped with the statue, and it now rests in a crypt on Kabruk's island."

"If this Philoctes could steal the statue, why did he not steal the book as well?" Sinbad nodded toward the grimoire.

"My father kept his darkest spells in his head, afraid that if he committed them to parchment, I would read and use them. Thus, there is nothing in the book that Kabruk has not already learned. For the same reason, I cannot simply strike out at him. He knows what I know, I know what he knows. As with two like poles of magnets, we would simply repel each other without effect. Neither of us can harm the other. My father's secrets would tip the scales of power, and Kabruk would destroy me and plunge the world into chaos. I must recover the statue before he finds the way."

"And where is Kabruk's island?"

"To the east in uncharted waters."

"And how will I find it?"

"Plazzo will guide your way. If you succeed in returning the statue to me, your rewards will be great."

Vatlek waved his hand, and the wall behind him shimmered away. Sinbad saw himself lying on silk pillows being fed by nubile maidens. All around him, chests overflowed with gold and jewels.

Vatlek's brows tilted toward each other, and his dark eyes became slits. "And if you fail?"

The scene dissolved into a fiery pit where Sinbad stood chained to its floor, screaming in pain and terror as winged demons swooped in and tore at his flesh with their clawed hands and feet, only for him to heal and be rent again. The blink of an eye, and the vision faded.

"Bring me the statue, Sinbad, and you will avoid eternal torment. And if, in the midst of this adventure, you should kill Kabruk, your rewards shall be even greater."

"He can be killed?"

"Each of us is mortal, some are simply less so than others. Plazzo will accompany you. He is not essential to me, but useful, and I shall be displeased if he comes to some violent end, so see to it that he does not. I see your thoughts. You are cursing him for tricking you into coming here. Do not. Plazzo merely acted as an extension of my will. You were mine from the moment you slipped that ring on your finger. Instead, curse me—if you dare." Vatlek faded into the grey mist with a last echoing whisper, "Good fortune, Captain." and he was gone.

Sinbad's mind spun. He realized that wizardry had overridden his common sense and tricked him into accepting Plazzo's challenge. If Vatlek spoke truth—and Sinbad had no reason to doubt it—he was as cornered by Vatlek as Plazzo had been by Samson on the deck of the Blue Nymph. He had no way to move but forward, and no escape from the predicament save success.

"I see the Master has concluded his conversation." Plazzo stood in the doorway, wearing a coarse-weave brown robe whose hood concealed his stubby horns. Snakeskin slippers hid his webbed toes, and he held his arms across his paunch, either arm to the wrist in its opposing sleeve to hide his batrachian hands. "Shall we go, Sinbad?" Gone was the plaintive tone, replaced by authority and self-assurance.

Sinbad looked around himself a last time. "Yes. Let us go. I hope never to enter this room again."

"For your sake and mine, I hope that you enter it one last time—with Vashwal's statue, or we all may be lost."

Sinbad followed Plazzo down the twisted corridor like a man in a waking dream. At one of the magic windows, Plazzo drew aside the drape. Sinbad saw the harbor once again, but this time, the glass was gone. He smelled the salt air and felt the offshore breeze on his face.

"Come," Plazzo said, and made to step through the casement.

"We will fall to our deaths. It is too great a height."

"Would Vatlek have us die before our quest has even begun? Step through with me."

Sinbad closed his eyes, took a long breath, and put a foot over the sill. Instead of empty air, he felt solid ground. He opened his eyes and saw the masts of ships swaying with the waves, the Blue Nymph's among them. Only then did he breathe again.

"Why did we not use that portal to enter the palace, Plazzo?"

"Because the untrained mind can absorb only so much at a time. Too much magic at once, too much challenge of perceived reality, can fracture the strongest intellect. I had to introduce it to you gradually, lest you lose your faculties and be useless to Vatlek.

Returning to the Blue Nymph, Sinbad's mind was filled with one thought: how to break the news to his crew. They would follow him into any battle, sail the most treacherous seas without hesitation, brook any adversity, but he could not, in good conscience lead them blindly into the perils of the blackest magic.

Sinbad and Plazzo reached the Blue Nymph's berth without incident. But instead of blowing a kiss to the mermaid on her stern, Sinbad turned his face away, ashamed of the perils the ship would endure, her along with it.

"Wait here, Plazzo," Sinbad said at the foot of the gang plank. He boarded the Blue Nymph but did not feel the same comfort at her rise and fall he had before. He felt a sense of guilt at the thought that the wizard's quest would endanger her as much as himself.

The crew were ordered to return by half-night, but a few had done so already. Like the father of children who came home before their curfew, Sinbad wondered what mischief had necessitated their early return.

Omar was squinting at a chart overflowing the table in Sinbad's cabin. He glanced up and knew at once by the look on his Captain's face that something was amiss.

"Put that chart away, my friend," Sinbad said. "We will not be sailing southward after all."

"No? Which way, then?"

"East."

Omar nodded. "East it shall be, Sinbad. Do I want to know the reason why?"

"I would say not, but to your misfortune, you must."

For the next few minutes, Sinbad told the story of the sorcerer's ruse that placed him between the proverbial Charybdis and Scylla. Omar listened, frowning more deeply as the account went on. When Sinbad finished, Omar sighed deeply. "So, you grabbed a kraken by its tentacle, and the other nine have wrapped themselves around you."

"Yes, that sums it well."

"I ask myself why Allah punishes me with such travail, then I look back at my life and realize that it all is justified. Of course I will sail your ship. You, I could likely live longer and happier without, but I could no more part with the Blue Nymph than drown myself in the sea. You say East. Perhaps you could be more specific."

"Plazzo will provide direction. I will call him on board now."

"I will sail on this damnable quest," Omar added, "but I cannot speak for the crew."

"I will give each his choice. I would force no one into such danger."

"So be it." Omar extended his hand and clasped Sinbad's wrist as the Captain's fingers closed over his.

"To the edge of the Earth," Sinbad said.

"To the edge of the Earth."

Sinbad leaned over the rail and called to Plazzo, who stood away from the gang plank, arms folded in the sleeves of his robe, hood drawn about his face. To Sinbad, he seemed unnaturally still, not so much as a thread of his garment moving in the offshore breeze. At the sound of his name, the apprentice raised his head, and Sinbad saw the glowing green of his eyes in the shadowed folds of his hood.

"Yes?"

"Come aboard."

Plazzo climbed the gang plank and as he stepped on the Blue Nymph's deck, Samson caught sight of him. The grey cat hissed and bolted to the furthest corner of the ship. Samson was fooled by Plazzo's disguise earlier, but seeing his true form, the cat was no longer deceived and knew all too well by his animal instinct the danger that the wizard represented.

By half-night, all the crew had returned, ready to prepare for a dawn departure. Omar assembled them on deck, and Sinbad stood by the helm where all could see and hear him. Plazzo stood at his left hand, and Omar at the right.

"My friends," Sinbad began. "We have sailed on many quests, braved many hostile lands, survived the stormiest seas, but this night, I stand before you to ask—not order—to ask that you accompany me on a journey that may prove more dangerous than any we have undertaken before. We will sail seas uncharted to reach an island on no map, the island of a sorcerer, and there I will perform a task that means my life to succeed."

At the word "sorcerer," murmurs broke out among the crew. Sinbad waited for the muttering to die down before he continued. "This is Plazzo. He will accompany us on our journey." The sorcerer's apprentice nodded acknowledgment. "He will serve as guide to our destination and ease our journey in what ways that he can."

"I smell magic on him," said Jair. "He is this sorcerer you speak of?"

"I would not lie to you, Jair. Yes, he is a wizard. But Plazzo is only the eyes and hand of he who impels me."

Again, murmurs rippled among the crew.

"I would never ask, let alone order any of you to do anything I would not do myself. An obligation has been laid upon me that I cannot refuse, and I ask you now to help me to fulfill that obligation and thus save my life. The perils may be great but so shall be the rewards of success. I ask you now to choose, and I will abide by your choices without prejudice. Should you agree to join me, step forward."

The crew was silent for a long moment, then Ralf spoke up. "We have all sailed with you for years, Captain. We have all saved each other's lives countless times. We all have all stood back to back against every foe, man, beast, or demon. For me, there is no other life. Where you go," He raised his axe above his head. "I follow." The giant Norseman took the step.

"Should I leave your side, Captain," Henri said, "where would I find such shipmates and such adventure? I am for you." The wiry Gaul joined Ralf, and right behind him, Tishmi, Rafi, and Byrne followed suit.

Singly, then in twos and threes, the crewmen joined them, until all had made the same choice. Sinbad's eyes teared at their devotion. "A man could not ask for better. Any thanks I offer will never be enough."

"You would do no less for us, Captain," Haroun said. He raised his fist. "To the edge of the Earth!"

The crew repeated Haroun's pledge, chanting it loudly.

"To the edge of the Earth! To the edge of the Earth!"

For the first time since he had left Vatlek's palace, Sinbad felt a glimmer of hope.

Dawn brought fair weather and good wind. The crew cast off, the main sail was raised, and the Blue Nymph once again rode the peaks and troughs of the sea. Omar approached Sinbad, who stood at the prow, gazing across the waves at the golden sunrise before him.

"Good wind, fair weather go well together," Omar said.

"Beneath the sky while the sun is high," Sinbad replied, taking a turn at the rhyming game.

"One must be brave to ride the wave."

"Leave hearth and home for shores unknown."

"Leave wife and child to explore the wild."

"That life is best that pursues a quest."

Omar shook his head. "I yield. You are more the poet than I."

"I have simply had more practice, old friend." Sinbad's expression turned

"TO THE EDGE OF THE EARTH!"

serious. "You have spoken with the crew. What is their mind?"

"They are resolute, Sinbad; they do not fear, but they are wary."

"As am I. I had to choose my words with care when I appealed to them. I have seen magic do great good, but I have also seen it work great evil." He looked at the emerald ring on his finger. "Vatlek has taken the luxury of choice from me. I must serve him or suffer everlasting agony."

"But the sorcerer also provides, does he not?" Omar said. "That ring. Does it really shield you from harm?"

Sinbad looked into the depths of the emerald at his finger. "It has already, but I must not allow its protection to make me reckless. Freedom from harm is brother to freedom from restraint. I cannot be harmed nor can the Blue Nymph because both are key to the success of the voyage, but any of you could be at any moment, and I must always take care to see that you are not."

Sinbad was quiet for a moment. "And there is always that one loose thread that can unravel the whole garment."

"Eh?"

"Vatlek said that one harm can come to me, and one only."

"And that is—"

"He would not say. Vatlek knows, and Plazzo knows, but I do not. It is a demon with a hammer that stands behind me every moment to strike me down if I stray from obedience."

"Like the heel of Achilles." Omar pondered the thought. "Wizards lie, Sinbad. After all, did not Vatlek use deception to draw you into this quest? Perhaps this threat is a painted devil."

"That may be so, but I would not take that risk lightly."

Neither spoke for a time, then Omar broke the silence. "Sinbad, you said sail east. It is a large, uncharted ocean we sail to find a tiny island with no name. To follow the sun is not enough. I need more direction."

Before Sinbad could reply, Plazzo spoke from behind them, startling them both. "I can remedy that."

"How long have you been standing there listening, wizard?" Omar snapped.

Plazzo merely smiled.

"You have a light step," Sinbad said. "You skulk as quietly about the deck as Samson. Perhaps I should put a bell around your neck to warn all that you are coming." With the sea and the deck under his feet, Sinbad felt his bravado restored.

Plazzo sneered. "Remember whom you serve, Captain." The last word bore a mocking emphasis.

"Whom *we* serve, Plazzo. We serve Vatlek equally."

"I am little more than extension of the Master's will. You would do well to remember that." Sinbad felt the ring tighten on his finger.

"But on this ship, my word is law. Challenge that, Plazzo, and you will be turning yourself into a fish to swim back to land, and I'll take my chances with your master. You would do well to remember that."

Plazzo nodded slowly. "Duly noted—Captain." The pressure of the ring eased. Plazzo turned to Omar. "Now, as for direction—"

The wizard drew his hands from his sleeves and held them before him as if cupping water from a pool. As Sinbad and Omar watched, a ball of swirling smoke appeared and coalesced into a glowing orb. Plazzo threw his arms up and out as one might launch a carrier bird, and the orb rose into the air above the prow. It moved through the sky ahead of the Blue Nymph. The crew stopped their tasks to stare and point at the glowing ball.

"Follow that orb. It will lead you to Kabruk's island—Captain."

Plazzo turned away and found a cask amidships where he sat, wrapped in his robe, unmoving.

"I see that Plazzo's gratitude for your part in restoring him was short-lived." Omar said, looking from the corner of his eye at their passenger.

"There is no gratitude where trickery is involved, only satisfaction."

"I am certain you would like to kill that web-fingered bastard, Sinbad," Omar muttered. "Say the word and I will with pleasure spare you the trouble."

"As would any of the crew. I cannot accept your offer, old friend, for he is key to this quest. Further, I am bound to return Plazzo whole to Vatlek or not only my life, but my eternal spirit be forfeit. He is, for certain, a dog, but he is, I regret, Vatlek's dog."

"I will be watching him with one eye."

"And keep the other on that orb. I have no doubt it will lead us true to our destination."

"I never learn," Omar grumbled. "I choose first and think later. Some day, I will say 'no' and spare myself much grief."

"That day would be sad one for us both, Omar."

"Indeed. Excuse me—Captain," Omar said, mocking Plazzo. "I have a ship to run."

Sinbad's eye settled on the orb, glowing brightly above the waves. I was right to put Plazzo in his place, he thought, but I must always remember that although he is only Vatlek's apprentice, Plazzo still commands some degree of magic. If he were to feel threatened in any way, there is no telling how he might behave nor what measures he might take.

On the sixth day of the voyage, the Blue Nymph was enjoying fair skies, and a strong wind drove her on course behind the glowing ball.

"Captain!" Haroun cried from his perch. "Sails! Red and black striped."

"How many?" Sinbad shouted.

"Five, six—no, seven."

"I know of no kingdom whose sails sport such colors."

"Pirates, do you suppose?" Omar said.

"That or a royal fleet, though I doubt that." Sometimes, a king or caliph would send his ships out to accost vessels to exact tolls from ships sailing near their coasts or seize sailors to man their own, but the Blue Nymph was so far from land, that a royal fleet was unlikely.

A moment later, Haroun called down from the aerie, "Captain it is not many ships. It is one, and it is on an intersecting course."

"One ship?" Omar said. "Seven sails?"

"To catch more wind than two or three. Greater speed."

"What ship could that be?" Said Fathi.

"A ship that we do well to avoid," Sinbad replied.

"If we have seen them, they have seen us," Omar said.

"Set an oblique course to starboard. If they turn, we will better know their intentions."

"Aye, Captain."

As the Blue Nymph turned its prow, Sinbad looked up and saw that their guiding orb now hung to port in the sky beside the ship. Sinbad realized that the orb was doubtless what attracted their pursuers to them. Where was Plazzo? Sinbad caught Byrne by the arm as he hurried by. "Find the wizard. Bring him to me."

"Aye, Captain."

"Haroun!" Sinbad shouted upward. "Does she turn?"

The lookout shielded his eyes with a hand. "Aye, Captain, she turns."

Now we know, Sinbad thought. Best to avoid battle and risk to the ship—and the mission. Time to run. "Full sail!"

The Blue Nymph was fast, but its pursuer, catching more wind in its many sails, was fast as well. Sinbad stood in the stern watching the adversary. The ship looked like a toy on the horizon, but each time Sinbad looked anew, the striped sails were just a bit closer. The ship was unlike any he had ever seen, a sleek hull but huge and unbelievably quick despite its size. A little sorcery might be a great help now.

Byrne returned alone.

"Where is Plazzo?"

"He is below decks, Captain. I thought he was sleeping, but I fear he is dead.

I tried all I know to rouse him. He seems to not even breathe."

"Do what you must to wake the web-fingered bastard. We need him now."

Through the afternoon, the Blue Nymph fled with all her speed, and the seven-sailed pursuer followed, slowly, inexorably closing the gap between them. And still Plazzo lay unmoving.

"At this rate, they will catch us before sunset," Omar said.

"The size of her," Sinbad said, "at least three times ours. How many crew, do you think?"

"I could not guess, but surely they outnumber us by many."

"We may not be able to outpace them, but a ship that size cannot maneuver as fast as the Blue Nymph. Luck and courage have saved us before."

"Yes, but we could use some help. That sleeping wizard is worse than useless."

"So, we must ply every wile that we know to escape."

Haroun shouted down from above. "Captain! Their prow is barbed."

Sinbad raised his glass to his eye and saw that instead of a standard bowsptit on the adversary, a barbed spear protruded from the prow. He could also see ant-sized men in the rigging and at the rails, no urgency in their movements, patient, confident.

"So that is their gambit," Omar said. "Ram their prey and hold them fast to board."

"Aye. We must use every skill to evade that end. When they get closer, we can use a slalom maneuver. It is more difficult to put a hook through a wiggling worm."

Sinbad looked again to the seven-sailed ship and saw deckhands at the bow laboring at what looked like a windlass. His breath caught when he realized that the barbed spear was not a bowsprit, it was a harpoon, and what the deckhands were cranking was a giant crossbow.

"Heel to port!" Sinbad shouted. "Show them our stern!"

"We cannot outrun them, Sinbad," Omar said. "That ship is too fast."

"Then make us the smallest target you can." He realized that was their best chance, but the thought of that fiendish harpoon piercing the breast of the mermaid all but brought tears to Sinbad's eyes.

The crew labored to pull every ounce of speed from the Blue Nymph's sails, but all took the time to arm themselves for the battle that was coming. Ralf stood in the stern brandishing his broadsword in one hand and his axe in the other, bellowing a challenge in his native language.

Henri stood beside him, an arrow nocked in his bowstring, waiting for the maurauders to sail the last inch into his range. Tishmi stood silent, her face betraying nothing as she watched the oncoming ship, her *katana* in her right fist, her *wakizashi* in her left. There would be blood this day.

A sound rang across the waves, like the twang of an impossibly large lyre. Behind the sound, the iron harpoon flew over the water, dragging an anchor chain behind it, and its barbed tip found the Blue Nymph's stern inside the curl of the mermaid's tail. The impact shook the ship, and immediately, Sinbad felt the drag.

In a moment, Haroun called down from his perch, "Captain, they are reeling us in."

Sinbad could see through his glass that their attackers were circling a capstan, pulling back the chain, and the Blue Nymph with it. On the attacker's deck, dark men with weapons assembled at the rail—a boarding party. Along the bow of the nameless ship, he could make out words carved into the planks in a language he did not know. He handed the glass to Omar. "Below the rail—words carved into the bow. Can you read them?"

Omar squinted through the glass for a moment. "It is the language of the Hindus. They are far from home."

"As are we,"

Omar studied the characters for another moment. "I cannot read it." Omar called across the deck, "Rahm!" The dark-skinned, turbaned Indian came to the rail. Omar handed him the glass.

"Words on the bow," Sinbad said. "The name of the ship?"

Rahm peered through the glass for a moment, then turned to Sinbad, his face grim. "She is called the *Kris*—the dagger—and there is more, not only her name, Captain, a boast, if I read it correctly." He sounded out the words: "*Ham kissee kaidee ko nahin lete.* We take no prisoners."

Ralf leapt from the deck, axe in his hand and caught the harpoon with the other, pulling himself up to straddle it as he swung his axe strinking sparks from the chain, but the taut links were too thick, their steel unyielding. He howled in frustration.

Sinbad slid down the ladder into the hold to find the barbed tip of the harpoon sticking through the bulkhead of the stern. He climbed topside again and called to Fathi. "Go below and try to pound the harpoon back through the bulkhead!"

"Aye, Captain!"

The Copt seized a long-handled maul and disappeared into the hold.

The distance between the two ships slowly, inexorably shrunk. "Prepare to be boarded!" Sinbad commanded. He could hear Fathi's hammer thumping into the iron-like teak below, but he knew it was too late. Their pursuers were already too close.

"It seems I woke at an auspicious moment."

Sinbad turned to see Plazzo standing behind him.

"Good of you to join us," Sinbad snapped, his voice laden with sarcasm.

Plazzo ignored him. The wizard stood silent a moment then bent over the rail. He pointed a finger at the chain, closed his eyes in concentration and shouted an arcane word. As Sinbad watched in amazement, a ball of blue lightning so bright that it pained his eyes to watch it ran up the chain. The water steamed around it as the fire streaked toward the enemy ship. Sinbad could see crewmen standing beside the capstan suddenly burst into flame. An instant later, the *Kris* exploded in a ball of fire.

Destruction was instant and complete. Debris rained from the sky all the way to the Blue Nymph, peppering her deck with chunks of wood, tatters of rigging, and striped sailcloth. An array of dark-skinned arms, legs and heads bounced on the Blue Nymph's deck amid spatters of gore.

Plazzo gripped the rail with both hands. His eyes closed as he took several deep breaths. He staggered to a wooden box nearby and sat heavily on it.

There was no shout of victory or even sighs of relief among the crew. All were stunned to silence by what they had witnessed.

"Our passenger has saved us," Omar said.

"But at some cost to himself," Sinbad replied under his breath. "He looks as if he might keel over any second."

"It was good that he was with us. We might not have survived that encounter."

"But if not for his presence, we would not be on this voyage and never have encountered that seven-sailed devil. The orb doubtless led the *Kris* to us."

"Aye, Plazzo is a curse unto himself, Sinbad. But for an apprentice, he seems to have learned quite well. Were I told of his deed, I would not have believed, but having seen with my own eyes, I can think only that it would not be wise to incur his anger."

"He will not act against us, Omar. To do so would counter Vatlek's wishes. He needs us and the Blue Nymph to succeed in this accursed quest."

"Aye, Sinbad, but what might he do when the voyage is ended?"

To that, Sinbad made no reply.

Freed of the drag of the *Kris*, the Blue Nymph once again sailed forward at speed. Omar looked over the rail where the chain still dragged behind them. "We will likely have to chop away at the hull with axes to rid ourselves of that chain. We cannot cross the Eastern Sea dragging a tail behind us."

"I would work at the hull from inside, not out," Sinbad said, pointing behind them where the fins of sharks, a voracious armada, already were gathered for their unexpected feast.

Sinbad looked again to Plazzo, whose chin sagged to his heaving chest, his face bathed with sweat as if he had just run a footrace. He is vulnerable now, thought Sinbad. I could throw him over the side and be rid of him. As if he heard the captain speak his thought aloud, Plazzo looked up. The wizard's eyes met Sinbad's, his mouth moved in a quiet word, and Vatlek's ring tightened on Sinbad's finger only long enough to serve as a warning.

It was sunset before the crew fully cleared the Blue Nymph of the grisly remains of ship and crew that had rained from the sky and swabbed her decks clean of blood. Heads, hands, and feet alike went over the side with the flotsam, and the sharks followed in the Blue Nymph's wake in such numbers that Sinbad wondered whether Plazzo had summoned them. He recalled Omar's comment and thought, if an apprentice wields such power, what might a master sorcerer do; not only Vatlek but Kabruk. How might he react to thieves on his island, in his palace? The thought chilled Sinbad's blood.

He went below where Omar supervised the patching of the ship's hull. The hole chopped around the embedded harpoon was larger than a man's head. It was above the waterline, but still demanded attention. The hole was too large for simple oakum and pitch. A sturdy plank from the *Kris* was cut to size and spiked to the bulkhead with a liberal slathering of hot tar to make the patch watertight.

"Not the prettiest job, but it will keep out the water," Omar said. "When we are in port again, I will find a carpenter to restore the outside, and none will know the ship was ever damaged."

"If I were a superstitious man, which I am not," Sinbad said, "I would worry at using a piece of so doomed a ship as part of our own."

"The magic was against them, not with them. I see it as simple salvage."

"Nonetheless, like a scar from a battle wound, a reminder of the darkness with which we deal."

Satisfied with the repair, Sinbad returned to the deck. The crew were all busy at their tasks, but gone were their songs and their laughter. Rather than rejoice at their deliverance, the sailors seemed to labor in fear that the forces that destroyed the *Kris* could as easily be turned on them. Battle, all understood, hand against hand, steel on steel. Sorcery lay beyond their simple grasp.

Sinbad went man to man, offering encouragement and praise for their performance under duress, but his words felt hollow because of the sense of unease the encounter and its outcome created in him.

For two more days after the encounter, the Blue Nymph followed the glowing orb as each night, familiar stars fell further behind them, and new, strange constellations swam into the night sky. Fair weather favored the ship's progress for a time, but the wind died down to a gentle breeze that scarce fluttered the Blue Nymph's sails. The calm continued for three days while the relentless sun blazed without mercy on the crew. The ship's store of water ran low, and rationing became the order of the day. Below decks the heat was unbearable, so the crew sat as still as possible in what shade could be found on the deck.

"Perhaps you could ask our web-toed passenger to blow in the sails and move us along," Omar said, wiping sweat from his brow.

"It seems there are some things even sorcerers cannot accomplish."

The first mate's face turned serious. "We need to land soon to take on fresh water, Sinbad," Omar said. "Perhaps you could ask Plazzo to send his orb to find it for us."

"Only if I must." Sinbad replied. "I feel that any gift from him becomes an obligation. But, he needs water to drink as do we all. I will wait for him to offer."

"I would say, do not wait much longer."

Later that morning, the winds returned, and the ship once again moved on the water.

The sun was tipping west when Haroun called down from his perch on the main mast. "*'Ard*!"

Land.

A moment later, "*Jazira*!"

An island.

Sinbad looked up from the helm in the direction Haroun pointed. He shielded his eyes with his hand. He said to Omar, who joined him on the bridge, "Damned if I can see it."

"You need the Monkey's eyes and his altitude."

"Follow his finger. It is the first land we have found in days, and it may be a chance to replenish our water, perhaps even find provisions. A fresh mango would please me right now. Set a course by Haroun's finger."

"So, I shall."

Haroun's eye was true. Shortly, Sinbad saw from the prow of the ship first, a tiny speck on the horizon. It grew as they neared it into a green mound and finally a sizeable mass.

Sinbad studied the island through his glass. A mountain dominated its center, sloping sharply to shore with flat land surrounding it like the brim of a peaked hat. The whole was covered in lush green vegetation. The surf broke on jagged rocks that protected a narrow strip of tawny sand, the only beach he could see. White birds circled overhead.

"What do you think, Omar?" Sinbad said, handing him the glass. Omar squinted through the eyepiece. "Lots of green. That means water. Many birds nesting in the rocks. That means flesh to cook and eggs to take with us." He handed back the glass. "I see no sign of men."

"Nor have I seen a soul. But we have been surprised before."

"Aye. Like the time we landed on that island off Madagascar and found it was the secret refuge of a crew of el-Kalifa's reavers. We were fortunate to escape."

"Not much of a beach on this side, at least. We could sail around it, see it from all sides, but by the size of the island, I would say that would take a half day or more. By that time, it would be night."

"I agree."

Sinbad weighed the alternatives. Caution cost time and lost the argument. "Gather the crew. We'll anchor a little closer and take the long boat ashore."

"Aye."

Soundings were taken half a league from the rocks, and the depth of six fathoms was determined. "I would not risk taking the Blue Nymph any closer, Sinbad," Omar said. "Rocks like those you see may be hiding offshore."

"Drop anchor, Omar," Sinbad said. "We can row from here."

Sinbad took his fighters ashore, leaving Omar with the rest of the crew aboard the Blue Nymph along with Plazzo, who sat on the deck on a coil of rope, lazing in the sun.

"We should take him with us," grumbled Ralf, loading an empty cask into the long boat. "He shares in the benefit. He ought to share in the rowing."

"I'd just as soon spend as much time away from that web-fingered devil as I can," Henri said, setting another barrel in the stern. "He makes my flesh crawl to look at him."

As always when they landed on a strange shore, Sinbad's landing party came armed and ready for whatever they might meet; Henri his bow and quiver, Ralf his axe, Tishmi her trio of deadly blades. The crew pulled on the oars with Sinbad at the tiller, and soon they were carefully navigating through the tall rocks that rose like conical spikes between the ship and the beach.

The nesting birds squawked in protest and flapped away at the invasion of their rookery, returning to the rocks once the long boat beached on the shore.

"We will first trek inland and look for water," Sinbad said, "then return for the casks once we find it. As green as this island is, we should find it soon enough. Byrne, you stay here and guard the boat."

"Aye, Captain," the Scotsman said. He reached under the bench where he'd

"WE'LL ANCHOR A LITTLE CLOSER..."

been rowing and pulled out his bagpipes. "That'll give me a chance to play m'pipes, since no one wants to hear them aboard ship."

Henri laughed. "If we get lost in the jungle, we can follow that screeching back to the beach. They are good for something after all."

The party plunged into the jungle to the shrill sound of skirling that was quickly lost as they pressed deeper inland through the dense tropical foliage. They found no ready path and had to hack their way through the rope-like Monkey Brush vines and ferns taller than top of Ralf's head. Ten feet was the limit of vision in any direction. Clouds of mosquitoes buzzed around their heads, and more than once the silky webs of spiders as big as an open hand barred the way.

Colorful birds darted from branch to branch like bright silk kerchiefs blown by a playful wind, calling to each other in a raucous chorus. The party broke through the heavy foliage to find a small waterfall that cascaded from the mountainside and poured into a pool whose overflow ran into the jungle and toward the ocean.

"There it is," Sinbad said. "No scum or debris on the pool. He cupped a handful and studied it in his palm. "Clear as glass." He sniffed it and offered to Ralf who did the same. "No odor that I can smell, Captain." Sinbad dribbled a few drops on his tongue. "No taste, either. It seems healthful enough, although I am sure Rafi would insist we boil every drop to be safe. Let us go back to boat for the casks."

The return to the long boat was much easier, since the travelers had hacked a path through the dense growth. The party was almost to the beach when the chatter of the birds ceased like the closing of a door. Sinbad held up a hand for them to stop. "Something is wrong. He drew his scimitar. Be ready."

The party closed into a back-to-back formation and drew their weapons, eyes peering into the green tangle around them for any movement, ears straining for any telltale sound. In a moment, a coppery face appeared, and a naked savage emerged like a ghost from the undergrowth. He stood a little over three cubits tall, less his black hair, which he wore pulled up in a thick bun laced with feathers on the crown of his head. The face below the sloping brow showed eyes like dark pebbles unnaturally close to either side of his flat nose.

He was no pygmy, but the shortest of the landing party stood a head or more taller than he. The native's every muscle and tendon stood out under his taut skin as if he had been flayed. Clutched in one bony hand was a short spear with sharpened bone as its tip.

Sinbad stared eye-to-eye with the newcomer for a few seconds, each taking the other's measure. The native let out a sharp bark, and the forest around the party came alive. A score or more of the coppery little men moved noiseless from concealment, encircling Sinbad and his crew. Their spears were raised and ready.

"Steady now," Sinbad said to his crew.

"We can take them, Captain," Ralf said.

A native stepped forward, and Sinbad discerned that this was their chief. Unlike the others, he wore a necklace of bones strung on a leather thong.

"We may not have to." Sinbad smiled broadly and raised an open hand. He spoke greetings in three languages. The ugly little chief's expression did not change. Like a striking snake, his arm whipped around, and his spear flew at Sinbad's heart. It stopped short and fell to the ground at Sinbad's feet. Sinbad realized that Vatlek's's ring protected him from the savages' spears, but his friends were in mortal peril.

The bewildered look on the Chief's face would have been amusing were the situation not so dire. Fearful murmurs broke out among the tribesmen. The chief grunted a command, and another native stepped from behind him, the tribal witch-man.

The witch-man wore a neck piece of bright feathers, and his face and torso were decorated with ceremonial scars in swirling patterns. Instead of a spear, he carried a staff capped with a human skull. He began a keening incantation and jerked about in a sort of dance, shaking his staff at the trespassers. He ended his gyrations by throwing back his head and wailing at the treetops to his savage gods.

Satisfied that the intruders' protective spell had been broken, the chief barked a Command, and the tribesmen raised their spears, waiting for his word to throw. Tishmi took a combat stance, *katana* in one hand, *wakazashi* in the other. Henri drew his bow, aiming an arrow at the Chief's throat. "On your word, Captain. He dies first." Henri was about to launch his arrow when a new sound filled the jungle, a droning like a giant swarm of bees. The chief and the witch-man looked at each other, whites showing at the edges of their eyes. The shrill keening of Byrne's chanter echoed through the trees.

To a man, the savages ran screaming in terror, many dropping their spears as they ran, the witch-man and the chief among them. In a moment, the skirl ceased and the hum of the drones died down. Byrne strode into view, bagpipes under his arm.

"We'll done, Byrne," Sinbad said.

"I heard the caterwauling of that heathen shaman. The pipes have sent the Picts a-runnin' more than once, and I figured they would do the same with this bunch."

"Play them all day if you like," Henri said. "I'll never complain about them again."

"We had best get back to the ship," Sinbad said. "We can seek water elsewhere. Our friends here were frightened, but that fear may not last long." In moments, Sinbad and the crew were pushing the long boat into the water and rowing through the rocks.

Pulling an oar, Ralf looked back to the island and said, "Captain, we had best pull harder."

Sinbad looked starboard and saw a small fleet of dugout canoes, the stunted natives paddling furiously in attack, and closing quickly on the long boat. Sinbad took Henri's oar as the archer stood in the stern, nocking an arrow to his bowstring. The nearest dugout was twenty fathoms away. Henri waited, calculating distance and allowing for the bobbing of the long boat and when he was ready, he fired, sending an arrow into the chest of a native who fell sideways from the canoe into the water, still clutching his paddle.

The faster dugouts were closing on the long boat. Henri fired again and again, sometimes hitting his targets and sometimes not. The first spear splashed into the water beside the long boat. Another flew through the air, and Tishmi's arm shot out like a striking cobra to catch the shaft in her hand and stop it an inch short of Henri's torso. Rather than throw the spear back and re-arm the thrower, she cast it over the side.

One of the dugouts drew close, and one of the tribesmen, a stone knife in his teeth, crouched to spring. He launched himself into the air, but before he could land in the long boat, Ralf swung his broadsword two-handed and cleft the little man cleanly in two. His lower half fell into the sea, and his upper half landed, twitching wildly, across the thwart. Ralf grabbed a handful of the shaggy hair and pitched the torso, its entrails hanging, after its legs. The natives frantically paddled away from the long boat and out of reach of Ralf's blade, but not before Henri put an arrow through two of them.

Over his shoulder, Sinbad saw the Blue Nymph, closer with every stroke of the oars. When he looked again, he saw Plazzo at the rail. The wizard held out his arms and waved them in broad circles. The sea gathered between the long boat and the dugouts and rose up in a giant wave that closed over the native canoes and swept them under.

In moments, the long boat reached the ship and the crew climbed aboard. Sinbad looked back toward the island and saw no trace of their pursuers or their canoes.

"The sea has them now," Plazzo said at Sinbad's elbow, in the same matter-of-fact tone he might have used to say that the weather was warm or the strap of his sandal needed adjusting. "I could not allow them to interfere with our mission." That said, he walked away leaving Sinbad staring after him.

That night as they ate, Rafi was full of questions about the tribesmen. "You say their eyes were close together?"

"That they were," Ralf replied. "And their foreheads slanted like a gang plank."

"Inbreeding, no doubt," Rafi said. "Possibly a ship sunk near the island stranding its crew for generations."

"A crew I can understand," Omar said, dipping his bowl again into the stew pot. "But to breed, they need women. Where did they come from?"

"I have known captains to take whores with them on long voyages to pacify the crewmen," Sinbad said, "defying foolish superstitions about women on a ship."

Tishmi rolled her eyes.

"That may be the case," Rafi said. "You saw a score of them but surely there are more. How many generations must they have been there to multiply into so many, and to descend so completely into barbarism?"

"I ken we will never know," Ralf said. "I for one hope never to set foot on that island again to ask them, if by now they even remember."

Omar looked around. "Where is the wizard?"

"Plazzo went to his pallet some time ago," Rafi replied. "He said he was tired."

"Too tired to eat." Sinbad considered this and recalled that Plazzo once again needed rest after plying his magic. He is made weak by it, Sinbad thought, but how weak? If he expends his power to get us onto Kabruk's island, will he still be able to protect us from Kabruk himself, or his minions?

Within a day, Haroun sighted another island, this one smaller than the last, but every bit as green. The Blue Nymph dropped anchor in a cove and the long boat was lowered. Sinbad elected to stay on board the Blue Nymph while Omar led a party ashore to search for water. Omar found no shortage of volunteers for the chore.

Sinbad took advantage of the quiet moment to approach the wizard who sat eyes closed, legs crossed and palms up in the stern.

"We have been at sea for thirteen days, Plazzo. How much longer must we follow that orb?" He pointed with his chin to the ball of light hanging at mouth of the cove, beckoning the Blue Nymph back to the deep water.

Plazzo sighed, his meditation interrupted. His green eyes met Sinbad's. "Impatient, Captain?"

"I simply need to know, as does my crew."

"Not long."

"How long?"

"Another day, perhaps two, and we will arrive at Kabruk's island." Plazzo smiled. "Then your mettle shall truly be tested."

"And how—"

Plazzo closed his eyes once again, and Sinbad realized the conversation was over.

Sinbad heard the long boat coming before he saw it. Balthus was singing the verses of a bawdy song and his mates joined in the chorus as they pulled at the oars:

"Fatima, Fatima, the woman is so wild,
That every year she gives a different man another child."

Their renewed spirit gladdened their Captain. For the moment, at least, the pall that Plazzo's sorcery had cast on the voyage seemed to have lifted.

Lines were thrown, and the long boat was tied to the Blue Nymph. Omar was the first up the rope to the deck.

"From the sound of things, I would guess you were successful."

"Aye, Sinbad. We found fresh water. The kegs are full. And there is more." Omar reached into his tunic. "Fresh fruit." Omar held out the red orb of a pomegranate the size of Sinbad's palm.

Sinbad turned the fruit over in his hand. "Wonderful." He opened his mouth to take a bite. The pomegranate suddenly flew from his hand, across the deck, and over the side where it splashed into the ocean.

"That is not for you, Captain," Plazzo said behind him. Sinbad turned to find the wizard in his customary pose, hands up his sleeves, and his hood over his brow.

"What—?"

"Vatlek told you that only one thing in this world could bring you harm. Knowing your experience with Persephone, goddess of the Underworld—that she gave you your magic dagger—the Master thought it appropriate that the fruit that chained her to Pluto's dark kingdom be your bane as well. To taste that pomegranate would result in instant death.

"It is unfortunate that this incident has forced me to reveal that secret, but I could not allow you, even by accident, to destroy yourself and the quest with it. Be warned." Plazzo turned away and went back to the stern, where he returned to his meditation.

Once he was out of earshot, Omar said, "So, the serpent is hatched from the egg. At least you now know that which can harm you. Many pardons for my unknowingly putting such fatal temptation in your path."

"No forgiveness necessary, old friend." Sinbad rubbed his chin. "It is better to know than not." He looked out to sea at the direction the pomegranate had taken. "But after thirteen days of fish and barley the sweetness of the fruit would be almost worth the price."

Two more days and nights, and the next morning, Haroun once again called out, "*Ard!*"

Sinbad strained his eyes to see a bump of land across the waves; its features shrouded in mist.

"Our destination, Captain," Plazzo said, unexpectedly at his side. "Kabruk's island." The wizard gestured, and the orb returned to his outstretched hands and disappeared. "We have no need of that now. Further, it would announce our presence if Kabruk does not already sense it."

"He knows we are here?"

"Perhaps. Like the spider feels the twitch of its web when a fly alights, an adept may feel the disturbance of the very air around him. This is close enough for your ship. We will take the long boat ashore, and if Fortune favors us, we will land unnoticed."

"When you say 'we,' Plazzo, whom does that include?"

"A half dozen of your choice to row. Make them fighters and fearless, Captain. Vatlek's ring makes you invulnerable, but I require protection. I do not know what may guard Kabruk's island, but it is no doubt formidable."

Sinbad recalled the Guardians of Vatlek's palace with a shudder. He balked at risking the lives of his crew, but he realized that once off the Blue Nymph and on the island, his authority ended and Plazzo's began.

"Do we wait for night?"

Plazzo shook his head. "We do not. The mist that shrouds the island will serve for stealth as well as would darkness. And what we may encounter there are things better seen than not."

Sinbad called to Omar, "Prepare the long boat." He looked again to the mist-shrouded island and wondered, once he left the Blue Nymph, would he ever tread her decks again?

As the crew lowered the long boat into the water, Sinbad pulled Omar aside. "Once we are out of sight, sail a good distance away to the north. If I do not find you by the third sunrise, flee. However this encounter ends, one wins, one loses. I do not want Kabruk's wrath nor Vatlek's visited upon you, the crew, and the ship."

"Aye, Sinbad. As you command." Omar chuckled in spite of himself. "Leave Haroun. He will see you a day before the rest of us, but in all the years we have been together, we have never failed to come home to port together. I will do as you say. I will sail north and wait three days. You are the stone that Allah has placed in my kidney to punish me," he said with a laugh. "I believe that Himself will not allow you to be removed so easily." The pair caught each other's forearms. "To the edge of the Earth," Omar said.

"To the edge of the Earth," Sinbad repeated. "Perhaps we have not found it yet."

"As we shall see."

Sinbad chose six to accompany him and Plazzo ashore: Ralf, Tishmi, Henri, Fathi, Jafari, fighters all, and Rafi—who knew what wounds might need tending? As they rowed away, Sinbad sat in the stern of the long boat. He cast a longing look back at the Blue Nymph, her sails filled, already sailing northward, then turned his face toward Kabruk's mist-curtained island and the hellish mission ahead of them all.

The crew pulled at the oars grim-faced and silent, no song nor chant on their lips. Their bravado was supplanted by wariness at dangers yet unknown.

"Is there a better place to land than another, Plazzo?"

"None less perilous. Kabruk chose his sanctuary well. I cannot say with certainty what we might find."

"For all his knowledge, Vatlek seems to have left you ill-informed."

"Just as the curtain of mist obscures the island, so does the sorcerer's spell hide the island's true nature, even from far-ranging eyes such as Vatlek's. We must see it with our own."

"Captain," said Fathi, "Sharks to starboard."

Sinbad looked over the side and saw the fins approaching the boat like the sails of an attacking fleet. A school of sharks had followed the Blue Nymph for days after the incident of the *Kris,* but had finally fallen away, realizing the bloody feast was ended. Here was a new armada of predators, larger than any of those that followed the ship, and larger than Sinbad or his crew had seen before.

The sharks swam closer, one of them rolling to its side as it passed the boat, its gaping mouth to show rows of jagged teeth. Sinbad felt a bump against the hull, and the long boat heaved. They were trying to tip the boat.

"Are these Kabruk's pets?" Sinbad said.

"It appears not," Plazzo said, his face impassive. "They are too ordinary."

The wizard offered no assistance, and Sinbad realized that he was saving his strength. To expend it now would leave him too weak to deal with whatever forces they encountered on the island.

"Captain?" Tishmi said, raising a eyebrow. She pointed to herself.

Sinbad nodded. "Fathi, hold her."

The burly Copt grabbed a generous handful of Tishmi's tunic with one fist and the thwart with his other as she leaned over the stern, offering herself as bait. A gray form flashed by its dead black eye measuring speed and distance. On its next pass, its snout broke the surface. Fathi pulled Tishmi backward, and as the finned devil's jaws snapped on the air, her razor-edged katana slit a hair-thin line along the shark's body.

The effect was immediate. Gore spread in the water, and the injured shark's companions, frenzied by the blood scent, abandoned their pursuit of the boat. The water churned red as they fell on their companion.

Tishmi dipped her blade in the water to wash away the blood and again took up her oar.

"Well-done, little one," Ralf said jokingly.

Tishmi gave him a withering stare. "In the trained hand, a hair pin can kill as surely as a meat axe, a quick finger as surely as a brawny arm. Death can be delicate. Someday you will learn that truth, Northman."

"She speaks truth, you know," said Fathi.

Ralf snorted and pulled at his oar.

As they rowed further, there was no gradual movement into the white mist. It surrounded the island like a keg, or a drum, flat on its top. One moment the long boat was outside it, the sky clear and the horizon visible; the next they were inside the white mass, and the rest of the world had disappeared.

The mist was cool on their skin after the harsh sun, but dry. Sinbad could see from the stern of the long boat to its bow, but little further. The mist also dulled sound. The dipping of the oars was all but silent. When anyone spoke, the mist muffled his voice as if he spoke into a pillow.

"This worries me, Captain" Henri said. "Our approach is muffled but so might be the island's defense."

"Which way, Plazzo?" Sinbad said at the tiller. "I do not steer well blind."

The wizard shrugged. "Straight ahead will do. The beach is not far."

Plazzo spoke true. In a few moments, Sinbad heard the distant sound of waves breaking on an unseen shore.

"Are there reefs, Plazzo?"

"How can I say? I have never been here before. The mist obscures my sight as much as yours."

"That glowing orb would be a help now," Ralf grumbled.

"And announce our arrival like a fanfare," Rafi said.

"Quiet now," Sinbad cautioned. "Listen."

The sound of the surf was louder now. Sinbad realized that the mist's dampening effect meant that the breaking waves were closer than perceived. "Steady now."

A moment more, and with no warning, the boat was lifted on the crest of a wave and hurled forward like a spear. As suddenly as the mist had engulfed them, the boat broke free of it, and Sinbad saw the white spray of the waves hurling themselves against a palisade of jagged rock. A narrow passage appeared, and Sinbad put all his strength against the tiller to aim the bow toward it. The rowers shipped their oars on the port side to keep them from splintering on the rocks as the boat scraped by. The long boat shot through the opening, and plunged into suddenly calm waters, a green cove.

The sudden calm was as disorienting as the sudden peril. Sinbad drew a long breath. The mist overhead blocked much of the sun, casting the beach and the jungle beyond it in a grey twilight.

Ralf and Fathi leapt over the side and pulled the boat aground on a beach as black as ebony.

"Black sand," said Rafi in wonderment. I have never seen black sand."

"Could it be ash?" Jafari said. "From a volcano, perhaps?"

Fathi scooped a handful of the black grains and let them flow between his fingers. "No ash, it is sand."

Sinbad and his crew climbed from the boat and looked around them. The black sand sloped gently upward to the edge of a jungle, which was as sharply defined as the border of the mist, and by all appearances, as dense. Vines, trees, and ferns formed a dull green wall that looked all but impenetrable.

Instead of looking into the island, Fathi gazed outward, the way they had come. "We will have the Devil's own time threading that needle in the other direction."

"Worry about tomorrow when it comes," Ralf said. "We have worry enough today. We—"

A hissing noise cut off his words. Slight at first, it grew quickly into a deafening susurration like the winds of a typhoon. Down the beach, the black sand swirled as if an invisible hand were stirring it, a small spiral at first, but growing ever wider until it rose into a towering black cone.

Sinbad and his crew stared in horror as the dark mass began moving their way. Blunt fingers of sand projected from the cone, reaching for them as they ran.

"WORRY ABOUT TOMORROW WHEN IT COMES."

"Back to the boat!" Sinbad shouted, but as if the sand heard him, its bulk shifted with a roll like a shaken sheet and hurled the long boat from the beach into the cove. The same roll threw the whole party to the ground, and they scrambled to regain their footing as the sand moved closer.

One of the dark fingers reached for Fathi and wrapped itself around him. Fathi screamed as it lifted him into the air to dash him to the ground. Ralf roared and swung his axe at the finger. It burst in a puff of blackness like smoke, and the Copt fell to the ground. Another finger formed to reach for Ralf this time, and another, and the Viking found himself swinging his axe in every direction.

Tishmi waded into the fight, spinning madly, arms swinging in sweeping loops, scattering the dark sand until it filled the air around her. But the longer the fight ensued, the more sand gathered.

Sinbad reached into his sash and drew Grachene, his dagger, Persephone's gift. Its blade glowed in his hand, and he knew what he must do. Sinbad ran at the black mass and threw himself into it headlong, holding the magic dagger ahead of him with both hands. In an instant, the black sand collapsed, and the fight ended, but Sinbad was buried alive beneath the mound.

He felt Vatlek's ring pulse on his finger. He was unharmed but trapped under tons of the dark sand. His arms held a small pocket of air around his face. Sinbad would have cursed, but his mouth was filled with the same dark grit as his nostrils. He tried to move, but the pressing weight held him inert.

Would he die thus? Would he soon suffocate? Or would the wizard's ring keep him alive, trapped in the black sand for all eternity? The thought horrified him, and he struggled to free himself, but could not move.

Let my last thoughts be of the Blue Nymph, the Blue Nymph, and the Blue Nymph, he told himself and filled his mind with the dream of standing on her decks, the wind filling her sails, her sleek hull gliding toward an endless horizon.

A strong hand grabbed his ankle, breaking his reverie. Another pair of hands seized his calf, and he felt himself being dragged out of the blackness. "He lives!" Sinbad heard Jafari say. The same hands pulled him to his feet as he spat out grit and gasped lungfuls of precious air.

"Are you all right, Captain?" Ralf said at his other side.

Sinbad raised his hands before him. "Let go my arms and we will see if I can stand unaided." Sinbad tottered a little at first but soon regained his balance. "I thank you both for rescuing me."

"Thanks to all, Captain," the harpooner said, his gold teeth glittering in a grin. It took all of our hands to dig you out."

"All but him," Ralf said disdainfully, casting a look at Plazzo over his shoulder. The wizard stood staring into the jungle, paying Sinbad's fate no mind.

Sinbad looked to his own hands still clutching Grachne. He had saved his shipmates, and they returned the favor. It was enough.

The long boat had capsized, but to their good fortune, had not sunk. It had drifted to the middle of the cove. "One of us will have to swim out to it," Sinbad said, "or we will all have to swim back to the ship."

"I will go," Jafari volunteered.

"We do not know what may lurk in those waters."

"Captain, I have spent my life at sea, and no creature has yet eaten me. I will go." The tall African stripped to his loin cloth and waded into the calm waters.

"Luck be with you," Rafi said.

Jafari turned and nodded to his companions, his gold teeth clamped around a long, wicked knife. He plunged into the cove and set out with powerful, even strokes, quickly reaching the boat. The stern reared out of the water. Jafari took a lungful of air and disappeared under the surface.

Sinbad and the others held their breath as well, agonizing moments, waiting for Jafari to reappear. A splash, and he broke the surface, a coil of rope over his shoulder. A breath, and he dove under once again to knot one end of the line around a mooring cleat in the bow and the other around his waist. That done he swam back to the black beach, bringing the line to shore.

All hands pulled at the rope, backstepping, and brought the boat to the sand where the crew righted it. "Luck is with us, Captain," Rafi said. "The boat seems sound, and only one oar missing."

"That would be my oar," Henri said with a laugh. "You will have to row to the ship without my back in it." Fathi began a joke about lazy Gauls, but Sinbad cut him off.

"Just as well," Sinbad said. "We may need your bow to shoot behind us." To Jafari he said, "Tie that rope to the stoutest tree it can reach. Whatever lay in that sand may be dead, and it may not. I want our exit ready when we come back. We may find ourselves in a hurry."

The word went unspoken but hung in everyone's mind: *If* they came back.

The boat was tied with double ropes to a sturdy tree at the beach's edge. Sinbad elected Rafi and Tishmi to stay at the shore to guard it and be ready to launch with no hesitation.

"So, Plazzo, yours is the tiller. Which way do we go?"

The wizard drew a red feather from his sleeve. He cupped it in his webbed hands and blew a breath on it. The feather rose into the air and drifted forward into the jungle. "That is our guide."

Sinbad followed the feather with his eye as it floated over the dense undergrowth. "It cannot find us a path to walk?"

"There is no path. You make your own."

The party set out, resigned to hacking their way through the dense foliage for as far as the feather would lead them.

No one spoke as they plunged into the jungle, making as little noise as possible. Absent were the common jungle noises, the cries of birds, the chatter of monkeys. The only sounds in the twilit forest were the occasional thrash of some unseen creature in the brush, and the constant whir of the mosquitoes that swarmed around them.

Despite the coolness of the mist, the crew soon found themselves drenched in sweat as they chopped through vines as thick as a forearm. In the lead, Fathi swung his scimitar at a vine that dodged away from its blade, and he found himself eye to eye with a serpent drawn back to strike, its curved fangs dripping venom. A flash of steel, and the serpent's head fell to the ground, its brown body writhing from a limb.

Fathi turned to Sinbad and whispered, "Many thanks."

Sinbad nodded acknowledgment, and the party forged on.

A sound ahead: running water. They came to a clearing where a rippling stream fed a pool as clear as glass. White stones shone on the bottom. Ralf bent to cup water in his hands to drink, and Plazzo said, "Hold."

Ralf eyed the wizard with irritation but obeyed his words. "Why?"

Sinbad said, "No fish, no newts, nothing alive in the pool."

"You are correct, Captain. And this is the reason." Plazzo pulled a frond from a nearby fern and dropped it into the pool. The surface bubbled and roiled around the fern as it withered to a husk then disappeared entirely.

"The poison in that pool would burn the flesh from a man's bones and given time, melt those bones like butter. Be wise. Nothing is as it seems here."

The absence of the sun above the mist made time-telling difficult and consequently, the trek seemed endless. Hours along, Plazzo finally held up his hand to halt. "From here, Captain, you and I will go alone."

"Based upon our progress so far with five blades, Plazzo, if I have to chop our way through this growth by myself, we may reach Kabruk's stronghold in a week."

"Have your crew cut away that stand of Monkey Brush." Plazzo gestured with his hand where the crimson feather floated in the air. The brush was the most dense they had yet seen on the island, its vines closely intertwined as if woven by a basket maker. Unlike its colorful cousins elsewhere, the flowers on these vines were a dim grey and the leaves a darker green than others of its kind. As Sinbad approached it, he realized that the brush formed a thick wall twice Ralf's height that disappeared into the mist to the left and to the right. It also was the most resistant to their blades.

"We do not need a road through here, simply a path," he said. "Work in pairs."

Ralf and Jafari were first, grunting and sweating as they hacked at the wall of brush and the others dragged the cut vines from the path. What resulted was a rough tunnel a fathom in diameter. Henri and Fathi relieved the pair while Ralf and Jafari guarded the path behind them.

Fathi was the first to break through, her razor-edged blades cleaving the vines as if they were ropes of clay. "Captain! I see light!"

The tunnel was already three fathoms long. Sinbad peered over the Copt's shoulder as he pulled aside a heavy strand.

Sinbad stared in amazement. On the other side of the brush-wall, the jungle was gone. A grassy meadow opened before him. Gone also was the mist, as if the woven wall of vines held it away. Colors were so vivid that they almost pained his eyes to look upon them. Flowers like none Sinbad had ever seen ran riot. Towering trees with crooked limbs clawed at the sky and cast shadows so black as to look painted on the ground. And at some distance, like the apex of a peak, Sinbad saw the blunt pile of stones that was Kabruk's palace.

"There is our objective, Captain," Plazzo said at his shoulder. "With my magic, your skill, and mutual good fortune, we will reach it and fulfill our mission."

"Only a part," Sinbad said. "If we succeed in stealing the statue, we must still get it off this island, and sail back to Kartesh to deliver it into your master's hand. I suspect that Kabruk will not take kindly to the theft and will use his arts to prevent that outcome. How far is his reach?"

"Far and wide," Plazzo said. "All the more reason for you to kill him—if you can."

Sinbad stared at the emerald ring. "This ring is proof against weapons, sharp and blunt, but will it stand before Kabruk's sorcery?"

"To that, there are no guarantees, Captain. Thus, it would be best you kill him as quickly as you can before we have to learn that truth."

In a short time, a passable opening was cut through the brush-wall.

Sinbad gathered his men around him.

"I go now to the most perilous part of this quest. I may not return. On the third sunset, wait for me at the shore. If I do not return by the next dawn, take the long boat and row due north. With luck, the Blue Nymph will find you."

"You will be back, Captain," Jafari said. "I have every confidence."

"You cannot fail," Henri added. "We have not yet found the edge of the Earth." The others murmured agreement,

"A man could ask for no better companions." And with those words, Sinbad turned away from his shipmates. The crimson feather bobbed through the opening, and Sinbad followed Plazzo through the evil hedgerow into a landscape undreamt.

Sinbad and Plazzo walked for what seemed hours across the grassy sward, but the stark shadows of the twisted trees were unaltered.

"The shadows neither lengthen nor shorten, Plazzo. How can this be?"

"Time slows to a near standstill within this boundary. The place is a nexus of intersecting forces. It is the secret to Kabruk's longevity. He is older even than the Master. While he remains here, he grows no older. But Slow Time itself is a blade with two edges. He has enjoyed its benefits for far too long. Should he leave the island, he will certainly age. The questions: how much and how rapidly. Will he return to aging at a natural pace, or will ten lifetimes descend upon him at once? That is why Kabruk desires the secrets of Vashwall. To protect him from such an outcome."

"Then he is a prisoner here?"

"Only of his own fear. Kabruk is loath to risk the unknown."

"So, I will not age so long as I am here?"

"You will not, nor will I, but my hope is that neither of us will remain here long enough for that to matter much."

"So, if time moves slowly, we will be in constant daylight?"

"For a considerable time."

"No night to conceal us, then. That will require great stealth."

"One of many reasons that you were chosen."

The red feather led a straight path across the grassland toward the palace, but as they trekked, the great pile of stone seemed no closer. Sinbad realized that not only was the distance greater than he imagined, but that Kabruk's stronghold must be far larger than it appeared.

A band of forest lay between the grassland and the palace, tall broad-leafed trees with leathery bark, the like of which Sinbad had never seen. He had to tilt his head to see their tops.

This was no natural forest. Their thick boles grew in rows, evenly spaced to form colonnades as geometrically perfect as any Sinbad had seen in the temples of Greece, like soldiers in formation. The branches entwined to form a green roof that all but shut out the sun. Stepping into the forest's green twilight brought relief from the heat, but not from Sinbad's wariness. The forest seemed to be a single living thing, as if all of the trees were of one mind, their roots joined beneath the soil. When one swayed in the breeze, all did likewise.

Sinbad divided his eyes between the forest floor, lest he trip over one of the snake-like roots that lay across the ground, and the branches high above, lest some unseen enemy drop from their height.

"The forest knows our presence."

Plazzo nodded. "Indeed, but not of our identity, neither our intention. To it, we are little more than lice on the scalp of a giant."

"If time slows here, as you have said, how long have these trees been growing?"

The wizard shrugged. "How old are the stars?"

A shrill whistle echoed among the thick boles. In the absence of bird calls, its effect was startling. An answering whistle came from behind them.

"Perhaps we should move more quickly," Plazzo said.

Sinbad drew his scimitar. He looked all around him but could see nothing save the great trunks of trees in any direction. Neither could he see Plazzo. The sorcerer had disappeared.

The duff in front of him erupted in a spray of dead leaves and rot. What sprang from the ground would have been a man save for its scaly copper skin, its yellow diamond-pupiled eyes, and a mouthful of jagged fangs that dripped what could only be venom. The creature was little more than skin stretched taut over bones. It hissed at him and charged, spindly arms spread wide, and claws ready to rend his flesh.

Sinbad's first stroke aimed for the monster's neck for a quick, clean kill, but the savvy creature twisted aside, deftly dodging the blade, and raked its claws at Sinbad's face, narrowly missing his eyes. Sinbad made a sweeping spin, bringing the scimitar around to cut through the flesh and parchment-thin bone of its thighs. The thing landed on its back, thrashing and spitting as dark blood oozed from the stumps of its legs.

"Behind you!"

Sinbad turned to see the forest floor heave as two more of the scaly devils burst from the ground. One rushed at him, and he thrust head on, impaling its chest almost to the sword's hilt. Sinbad felt claws dig into his shoulders as the creature tried to pull him to its maw. Its companion circled behind to strike at his neck, but Sinbad swung its body, lifting the still impaled monster off the ground, surprised at its lack of weight. Putting it between himself and its kin. He ran at the second lizard-man, pushing the impaled one ahead of him, forcing the attacker backward to trip over a tree root.

Sinbad planted a foot in the chest of the impaled reptile and kicked it free of his blade. The creature fell and did not move, the light gone from its eyes.

Its comrade had scrambled to its feet too close for a sword stroke. Two-handed, Sinbad brought the pommel of his sword down on the leathery skull and felt it crush like the shell of an egg.

Arms wrapped around his knees. The legless reptile had crawled behind him and was trying to pull him down. Sinbad kicked himself free of its grip and seized the creature by an arm. He swung it full force against the bole of a tree, hearing bones crack and bringing a gout of ichor vomiting from its maw.

Sinbad turned in every direction, expecting more attackers, but saw none. The forest was quiet again.

Plazzo came from behind the tree that hid him.

Sinbad glared at him. "Where was your help?"

"You seemed to need none, Captain. Further, I could have been injured. You could not."

Sinbad looked to the ring. The emeralds glow pulsed with the beat of his heart. At his shoulders where the creature had gripped with its claws, there was no blood. The skin was unbroken.

"Let us move on," Plazzo gestured toward the lifeless bodies. "There may be others."

With every step, Sinbad's eyes darted upward to the loftiest branches and downward to the ground around him, wary of any movement.

Plazzo followed the crimson feather, his face impassive, as if he had trod this path many times, merely a *cicerone* going through the motions to deliver Sinbad to his destination.

"This trek gives you no pause," Sinbad said. "No surprise. You have been here before?"

"Never. But what you have seen so far pales to feats of magic that I have seen Vatlek perform, Captain. When one sees marvels every day, his sense of wonder erodes quickly."

They trudged onward through the timeless forest. "Do you tire, Captain?" Plazzo inquired.

"No, to my amazement, I do not, though it seems we have been traveling for hours."

"The effect of Slow-Time, no doubt, although logic would dictate otherwise. You would think that normal movement in this place would be exaggerated to the point of excessive speed and hectic motion, but for reasons beyond my ken, it does not. Perhaps to an outside observer, it may seem so, but to us moving in this matrix, no. The eye of the observer, eh?"

"That is all very interesting, but limits exist to all things. We must tire eventually. How much longer must we walk this path?"

"Patience, Captain. Not long, even as you know time."

The regimented trees evoked an almost hypnotic effect on Sinbad, who, walking ten paces, saw a consistent view, the perfect ranks of trees disappearing into the distance that he had seen ten paces before. No obvious way existed to chart their progress. He tried counting the rows as he passed them, but having no end number, realized the futility of the tactic and abandoned it.

A whispering sound intruded on the forest's silence. It began as an almost imperceptible susurration and swelled to fill Sinbad's ears. He thought at first it was wind rustling the branches high overhead, then realized the branches were moving on their own.

"Hurry," Plazzo cried. "The forest is waking."

Sinbad looked to his feet, and saw the serpentine roots writhing, pulling from the earth and adding a ripping sound to the cacophony. They lashed at his legs like tentacles. Then Sinbad looked ahead of him and saw the huge boles shifting, inching together to close ranks in their path. He looked around him and saw the trees creeping toward them from all directions, slowly, inexorably, to trap them in a circle, or, he realized with a shudder, crush them between those massive trunks. Branches bent down and raked at them, but the trees were too tall to reach the ground.

"Hold onto my hood," Plazzo said, "and do not let go." Sinbad grabbed a fistful of the coarse weave. Plazzo muttered a spell, and Sinbad felt his feet leave the forest floor. They began to glide through the closing boles. Sinbad clutched Plazzo's robe with his left hand, and with his right, swung his scimitar at the clutching roots. One of them caught Sinbad's ankle and all but pulled him from his grip on Plazzo's robe. A stroke of the scimitar cleft the leathery bark and the fibrous pulp inside it.

Another root struck his torso like a cobra. Its tip did not impale him, but the force of the blow knocked the breath from his lungs. Still, he clung to Plazzo's robe, and still he gripped his scimitar and slashed at the writhing roots.

Ahead of them, Sinbad saw bars of light, like looking through the pickets of a fence. As they flew toward them, instead of growing larger, the bars of light were shrinking.

Plazzo cried out, a last desperate word and the pair shot forward, nearly pulling Sinbad's arm from the socket. They burst into the light as the thick trunks crashed together behind them with a thunderous boom.

The pair tumbled to the ground. Sinbad rolled and sprang to his feet, sword at the ready, but the deadly trees came no further.

Plazzo rose to his knees but could not stand unaided. Sinbad pulled him to his feet, where the wizard tottered, webbed fingers over his eyes. The red feather danced in the air before them, but Plazzo did not move. "I—I cannot—I must rest."

Sinbad looked around him at a barren landscape that looked as if the ground had been sown with salt. As far as he could see in any direction, an expanse of sickly yellow clay, bereft of any vegetation; neither a blade of grass, nor a leaf, nor a flower grew from its face.

"We cannot stay here in the open," Sinbad said, and unceremoniously threw Plazzo over his shoulder. The feather bobbed away, and Sinbad trudged after, carrying the wizard across the yellow expanse.

The clay was soft and as sticky as a spiderweb. It clung to Sinbad's boots and more than once threatened to pull one or the other from his foot. Plazzo was heavier than he looked, and walking with this burden slowed Sinbad's progress.

The sun, no longer blocked by the trees, shone harshly, and soon, Sinbad dripped with sweat. He looked behind him, and saw that his tracks were disappearing, the yellow clay closing over them like healing wounds, More wizardry. There would be no following of them to find his way out of this hellish place. More than ever, he realized the importance of keeping his companion from harm.

Plazzo did not move on Sinbad's shoulder. He would have thought the wizard dead, had he not remembered Byrne's attempts at waking him when the Blue Nymph was attacked by the *Kris*. Plazzo would wake when he woke, Sinbad decided, and until then, he could do no more than follow the feather and hope no attack came to force him to fight one-handed to keep them both alive. Ahead in the hazy distance, Kabruk's palace, its base shrouded in mist, rose like a small mountain.

With no gauge of time's passage, Sinbad was unsure how long Plazzo enjoyed his rest on one of Sinbad's shoulders or the other, but finally, a finger moved, a hand twitched. The wizard let out a long breath. His voice spoke in Sinbad's ear. "You may set me down, Captain."

"Gladly."

"I am restored."

"It is a good thing. I could not have carried you forever."

"As you have seen, my powers are substantial, but their force enjoys inconvenient limits. Thus, I must be judicious in its use. Depending upon how I employ it, it can be quickly spent, and I must rest to build it again."

"Then let us continue and hope such needs do not arise."

The feather bobbed away, and the pair followed after it across the desolate yellow expanse. Sinbad's eyes searched the sky. No birds flew overhead, and he was grateful, recalling the leather-winged creatures he had seen through the window of Vatlek's palace.

"Does Vatlek have a window that opens onto this place?"

"He does not. Kabruk's magic prevents that, else we could have simply stepped through it and arrived. But it is just as well. I can imagine, though you likely cannot, what horrors Kabruk might send through it in the other direction."

Sinbad shuddered at the memory of the Blue men fleeing the leathery birds and at the thought of those creatures pouring through Vatlek's portal, soaring over his palace walls, and feasting on the denizens of Kartesh.

"Yes. Just as well."

The shadows had not moved, or if they had, the distance was imperceptible to Sinbad. Still, Kabruk's distant palace looked no closer. Sinbad's eagerness for the trek to end countered his sense of unease at what unknown forces he and Plazzo must deal with when it did.

The feather stopped its forward progress, bouncing like a moth against a pane of glass.

"We are here," Plazzo said matter-of-factly.

"Here?" Sinbad said. "The palace is leagues away." He pointed to the monolithic heap of stone, which looked in the distance small enough to fit in the palm of his hand.

"As I have said, Captain, all is not what it seems." Plazzo closed his eyes and his brow creased in concentration. The air rippled before Sinbad's eyes, and a circle the size of his head opened in it like the parting of a whale's skin by the edge of a flensing knife. Through it, Sinbad saw the great blocks of the palace foundation a mere spear's throw away, stones the size of which he had seen in Athens' Parthenon and the great pyramids in the Valley of the Kings, making him wonder anew at what great force set them in place. As quickly as it opened, the hole closed, and the palace was distant once again.

"How?"

"You have a spyglass, Captain?"

"Yes, but—"

"Looking in one end brings the distant closer. What happens when you look through the other?"

"Things look farther away."

"Precisely. A force surrounds Kabruk's palace like a great lens, making it seem distant and inaccessible when it is not."

"So open that hole again and let us go through it."

"It is not so simple. My spell held it open for as far and as long as I could before the force closed it again. Even if I could open a portal large enough for you to step through, I could not guarantee its duration for you to pass to the other side. Should it close around you, you could be trapped for all time like a fly in amber."

"Then how—"

"There are many routes to the same outcome." Plazzo held out his hand and the red feather drifted to it. His fingers closed around it, and he pointed to the yellow clay at Sinbad's feet. It began to roil and bubble as if boiling, and

"WE ARE HERE," PLAZZO SAID.

to swirl like a whirlpool, funneling downward. Sinbad felt his feet sucked into the vortex, and with a startled shout he was pulled downward as the earth closed over his head.

He landed with an undignified thump in darkness in an open space; a cool floor, and when he stretched an arm, his fingers found an earthen wall. Another thump and Plazzo joined him. The wizard spoke a word, and a glowing orb like the one that guided the Blue Nymph appeared in his hand.

They stood in a featureless tunnel that stretched as far as the light would reach in either direction.

"You could have warned me, Plazzo."

"And what would your reaction have been despite any assurance when I told you would be pulled through the earth like an infant from its mother's womb and delivered into darkness?"

"After all I have seen on this quest, little would surprise me, let alone give me pause."

"Perhaps." Plazzo pointed forward. "This way."

"What lies in the other direction?"

"I do not know. To the sea, perhaps. Like all powerful men, Kabruk is not openly wary of those who might usurp him, but he is not so arrogant as to believe that none exist who exceed his power. This passage is one of many means of escape."

"Good to know. But what leads out also leads in."

"Spoken with the true wisdom of a thief. Let us go."

"Will we find our way unbarred and unguarded?"

"Perhaps, but you might wish to travel with your sword in hand."

The tunnel was wide enough for the pair to walk side by side, but Plazzo followed a step behind Sinbad, in case Kabruk had minions lying in wait.

The tunnel led to a barred copper gate, green with verdigris. As expected, it was locked.

"Time for your magic," Plazzo said.

The lock plate had a keyhole on the inside only, requiring Sinbad to reach through the bars to work his knife into it. After several attempts, he could feel the mechanism dragging the bolt back. It was all but clear when a snarling shape struck from the darkness on the other side and clamped its jaws on Sinbad's wrist.

The creature might have been a wolf were it not without legs and six cubits long. Its furred body coiled like a serpent around the copper bars, and it shook its head side to side, pulling Sinbad's hand away from his task. Its eyes glowed pure hatred. Its fangs did not penetrate Sinbad's skin, but the grip of its jaws was unrelenting, pulling him by his arm against the gate.

Sinbad gripped the hilt of his scimitar with his free hand and thrust it through the bars, but the curve of the blade made a straight attack difficult. Sinbad planted his feet against the gate and pushed with his whole strength, pulling his arm through the bars until the evil, furred head was against them. The creature arched backward with unexpected force, and yanked Sinbad against the gate, slamming his forehead against the green bars.

Black and white flashed across Sinbad's eyes, and he knew he must end this battle quickly. He twisted his torso as far as it could turn and swung his blade at the coils wrapped around the bars. One stroke cleanly cleft three of them. Sinbad, propelled by his legs, flew backward, dragging the truncated creature through the bars. Though half its length was gone, the furred thing kept its grip on Sinbad's wrist, its eyes glowing yellow. Its remaining body coiled around his arm in a crushing grip.

Sinbad struck the top of its skull with the pommel of his sword once, twice, and on the third blow felt the bone crack. Two more strikes, and the light left its eyes. But in death, the jaws retained their grip. Try as he might, Sinbad could not pull them apart with one hand.

"Plazzo, help me."

"I have no such strength if you do not."

"Your magic, then."

"The creature is of Kabruk's making. My limited powers cannot affect it."

Sinbad snarled and swung his arm, smashing the furred head against the gate again and again, pulverizing the bone until finally, it fell away. Sinbad's chest heaved with his breathing.

"Where magic fails, brute force prevails," Plazzo said. "The creature would have rent me to pieces."

"What was that thing?"

"One of Kabruk's creations. He remedies his boredom by transforming the natural into the grotesque. Now, Captain, the lock."

Sinbad took longer this time because his attention was divided between the task at hand and the darkness beyond the gate, wary that it would spew more horrors, but none came. The lock finally yielded, and the gate swung free. Sinbad hesitated.

"There is no way for us to go but forward," Plazzo said with a wave of his webbed hand. "We succeed at the quest or die, at Kabruk's hand, or at Vatlek's."

Sinbad stared down the tunnel receding into darkness beyond the glow of Plazzo's orb. A wizard who needs walls and gates and creatures to protect is not invulnerable, Sinbad thought. Vatlek's words: All of us are mortal. If so, then there is a chance that I may yet succeed, and a chance is all I ever have needed. As the old Roman proverb has it, *Ardentes fortuna iuvat*: Fortune favors the bold.

Summoning every ounce of his bravado, Sinbad plunged into the unknown with the Devil ahead and the Devil behind.

Omar watched the sun set for the second time since the Blue Nymph left Sinbad and his landing party on Kabruk's island. Sinbad's orders were explicit, but for the first time in all the years they had sailed together, Omar was ready to disobey them. He called up to Haroun at his perch atop the mast. "Any sign?"

The lookout strained his eyes and scanned the southern horizon, seeing nothing on the ocean's face. "None, Omar."

One more day, one more night, thought Omar. The crew were becoming restless, weary of busy work to keep idle minds away from worry. The Blue Nymph's decks were scrubbed clean as a dinner bowl. The smallest hole in her blue sails was stitched shut, and no speck of rust tarnished the links of her anchor chain. The ship was like a prize Arab stallion: snorting, pawing the ground, eager to race, poised to run at the starting gate, but reined back by its rider's hand.

One more day, one more night, thought Omar, as the rim of the sun dipped below the western horizon—and perhaps one more.

Across the deck, Omar saw Mufi lowering a net from the bow. Fresh fish would be welcome after days of salted meat. The wiry little man grinned. "Twenty fish!" He boasted. "A denarius that I will catch twenty fish. Who will take my wager?"

"You already feel the weight of your net," Daggot said. "Only a fool would take that bet." The others laughed. Mufi leaned over the rail to pull in his net. "The net is heavy. Who will bet thirty?"

"I will," said Arios the Greek. "Bring in your catch before another fish wanders into it."

Mufi tugged at the net but could not pull it from the water. "I need help."

Arios and Daggot started forward, but before they could reach him, with a startled cry, Mufi flipped legs up over the rail and disappeared from sight.

"Mufi!" Daggot shouted. He ran to the rail and looked over to see the laughing Arab dangling, one of his feet in the water, by a rope in one hand and his net bunched in the other.

"You should see your faces," Mufi said. "Pull me up."

"It would serve you right to leave you hanging there," Arios said, craning his neck over Daggot's shoulder. "Your jest is not funny."

"I say pull him in so that I might box his ears," Daggot said.

Omar looked over the side. "Bring him up."

The sailors pulled at the rope, and Mufi's face was almost to the rail, when something dark broke the surface and slashed across the bow striking the dangling crewman with such force that he lost his grip and flew through the air to splash into the water fathoms away.

Mufi bobbed to the surface, choking and gasping as a tentacle wrapped around him and pulled him under.

Before Omar could give an order, the rubbery arms of the sea beast whipped over the ship's rail from both sides. "Take up arms!" He ran to the stern and took up an axe, swinging it with both hands at a tentacle wrapped around the mast. To port, the monster's head broke the surface, and Omar looked into its luminous eyes.

The Kraken lifted the screaming Arios into the air and dashed him to the deck, then pulled his broken body over the side. The ship rocked as the beast tugged one way then another. The crew staggered back and forth, desperate to hold their footing as the tentacled horror tried to pull the Blue Nymph under.

The crew scrambled for any weapon available, and hacking, stabbing, or clubbing the deadly arms defended the ship and with her, their lives. The kraken's blood sprayed from dozens of wounds, but its tentacles held fast.

Daggot appeared at Omar's side, a harpoon in either hand. "The eyes!" Omar shouted. "Aim for the eyes."

Daggot drew back his arm and hurled his first harpoon. The tip bit into the fleshy head just a span above the left eye. He mouthed a prayer to his pagan god and threw again. This time, the blade struck the glowing eye, which sunk inward like a collapsing tent. Omar felt the ship shake as the Kraken shuddered with pain and anger. The tentacles pulled the Blue Nymph closer, and Omar saw malevolence in the kraken's other eye. He drew back his arm and sent his axe spinning through the air. Its edge broke through the eye's membrane, and ichor poured through the cut, staining the sea around it.

The kraken's grip on the Blue Nymph was unrelenting and Omar was certain that the ship was doomed. The Kraken would surely capsize her, and all would be lost.

From his post at the top of the mast, Haroun cried, "Fins!"

In the fading light, Omar saw them. The Kraken's blood in the water had drawn a school of sharks larger than any the mate had seen before. They harried the tentacled monster sweeping in to tear chunks of flesh from its arms and its body, turning the sea red, bringing more to share in the feeding frenzy. A tentacle slipped over the side, then another as the Kraken found itself to be prey, not predator. It lashed at the sharks, but the finned attackers were too swift. Another tentacle slid, limp, over the side, and another. The Kraken wrapped a tentacle around one of the sharks from the water, snapping at the air, and hurled it away as more attackers came and plied their jaws on the monster's flesh.

Soon, the Blue Nymph was free of the Kraken's grip, and the monster floated to port, the myriad sharks gorging themselves in a frightful feast. The tentacles flopped weakly, then ceased moving altogether.

The ship bobbed in the water as if nothing had happened. Omar looked across the blood-slick deck where the crew slumped in exhaustion. One more day, one more night. What terrors might they bring?

At the hedgerow, the crew waited. What few supplies had not been lost when the long boat capsized in the inlet were exhausted, and they were all hungry. In the meantime, the four were kept busy chopping at the green wall, which persisted in trying to grow shut the portal they'd cut before.

"I am so hungry I could eat the leaves off these damned vines," Fathi grumbled.

"From what I have seen of this place to now," Henri said, "I would fear to eat anything that grows here. It all seems tainted with wizardry."

"I'll take the chance." Fathi pulled a handful of the dark leaves from a fresh cut vine. He sniffed at them. "They have no foul odor." He put one in his mouth, rolled it around on his tongue, tasting it, and began to chew. "Not bad. Not delicious, but not awful either." He swallowed a mouthful and reached for more when a strange look twisted his face. Fathi clutched at his stomach and gasped in pain.

"Uh—Uh—" Fathi tried to speak but words would not come.

"Gag yourself!" Jafari said. "Vomit it out." When Fathi did not, Jafari pulled open his jaws to thrust a finger down his throat. He could not, because a clump of the grey vines burst out of Fathi's mouth like a clutch of tentacles and wrapped around his wrist.

Fathi's eyes burst and grey flowers bloomed as the vines sprung forth and wrapped around his head. More snaked from his ears and twined with the others, wrapping the Copt's head in a grey cocoon. He would have fallen, but the vines had burst from his toes and rooted into the soil.

Jafari wrenched at the vines around his wrist but could not free himself. Tishmi stepped forward and with one stroke, sliced through them. Even cut free, they clung to Jafari's wrist, and he could feel the sharp pain as they tried to root in his flesh. He drew his knife and slid the blade between his skin and the clutching tendrils, sawing at them.

More vines sprung from the tips of Fathi's fingers, winding around his wrists and climbing his arms. There was no blood. The vines had drunk it all. Leaves sprouted, and what had once been Fathi now stood before them, an obscene topiary.

Jafari cut away the vines from his wrist, and when they fell to the ground, they clutched like fingers, digging for purchase into the soil.

The three stared in horror at what moments before had been their shipmate and friend. White bone showed through the foliage; no flesh remained. They could hear ribs cracking as the deadly vines grew thicker and ground Fathi's bones together.

Henri turned to stare at the hedgerow and shuddered. "If this be how they grow, how many lives were lost to that barrier?"

I do not care about them," Jafari said. "I care about this life." He began sawing at the roots at Fathi's feet with his knife. "I will not leave Fathi here like this."

"Wait," Henri said. "Perhaps there is a better way." He gathered a handful of duff from the ground and striking flint to steel soon had fire. He tore a piece of cloth from his jerkin and wrapped it around a tree branch to make a torch. "It mocks our steel. Let us see how it likes our flame."

Henri held the torch to one of the Fathi-thing's outstretched arms, and the vines shrunk back, revealing what was left of the Copt's bones. Singed leaves gave off smoke that stung their eyes and offended their nostrils.

"Gather duff and wood around his feet," Henri said. "That is how we deal witches and warlocks in my homeland. It will serve as well here."

In a moment, a cone of wood ringed the base of the green horror. Henri bent to light the fire and Jafari said, "Allow me. Fathi was my friend."

"As you wish." Henri handed the torch to Jafari, who said, "It is nowhere near vengeance enough, but if it is all we can do, so be it. Farewell, my friend."

Jafari touched the torch to the makeshift pyre, and yellow flames curled from its base. The vines began to writhe, but entwined and rooted as they were, they had no escape as the fire climbed higher until the whole mass crackled in flame. The vines burned quickly, and in moments, naught was left save a mound of ash and a handful of broken bones.

Henri turned toward the hedgerow behind him. "They burn. I have half a mind to set this whole abomination ablaze."

"Not until the Captain returns," Jafari said. "He and the wizard need the opening to find their way."

"If he returns," Henri said, voicing the fear that had to that point been unspoken by all. "If he does not, I will burn this foul barrier to the ground."

The tunnel came to a juncture with another that branched to the right. "This way," Plazzo said, pointing to the branch.

"And where does this lead?" Sinbad said. The constant wariness wore at him as severely as hard labor, body and mind. He now carried his scimitar ready to strike at anything that might appear.

"To Kabruk's doorstep. It is not far."

Twenty paces further, and Sinbad felt a trickle of dirt on the crown of his head. Instinct took over. He seized Plazzo by his robe and threw him forward and quickly rolled after him, barely in time to avoid a block of earth that filled the tunnel behind them and that would have crushed them like ants.

"A dead-fall," Sinbad said.

"Quick thinking, Captain. Vatlek chose well when he chose you."

Plazzo's calm reaction to peril was fraying Sinbad's nerves.

"Does none of this shake you, Plazzo?"

"I will save my concern for what may come later." Plazzo pointed forward. "There is our entrance."

The glowing globe drifted ahead, and Sinbad saw a staircase, slabs of stone piled one upon another rising into darkness. He looked back to the blocked tunnel. Any hope of retreat and reaching daylight and the sea was dashed. Like a mouse in a drainpipe, he now truly had no way to go but forward.

Sinbad and Plazzo climbed the broad stairway, this time with Plazzo in the lead. The stones were rough under Sinbad's feet, not polished smooth by ages of traffic. By habit, he counted them as they climbed—knowledge to aid a retreat—twenty-one in all, to a landing surrounded by emptiness on all sides.

"What now, Plazzo?" Sinbad whispered. "There is nothing here."

"Nothing that you can see." The wizard spoke a few words in his arcane language, and the air seemed to shimmer like ripples in a pond. The rippling air resolved itself into stone walls, and a door, this one solid, not barred, and emblazoned with silvery runes and symbols.

"Kabruk's protective wards." Plazzo closed his eyes in concentration. His lips moved, but Sinbad could not hear his words. The symbols on the door began to move, revolving like constellations around the North Star, settling in a new arrangement.

"How did you know to do that?" Sinbad took a step backward, hand on the hilt of his scimitar. "Are you in league with Kabruk?"

Plazzo laughed without smiling. "How do you know how much sail and how much rudder catches the best wind to propel your ship, Captain? A coconut falls from a palm, never rises into the sky. Some spells are so commonly known and employed that the adept use them almost by instinct. Locks keep the honest out. So, spells do the unknowing." He pushed at the door with his webbed fingers, and it swung inward on silent hinges.

A breath of chill air came from within and seemed to coil itself around Sinbad's body, making him shudder. Plazzo cupped his palms and the glowing orb settled into them. He closed his hands around it, and in a breath, it was gone.

Though he saw no lamps, no sconces, no torches, Sinbad could see a dimly lit corridor ahead of them, walls hung with rich tapestries and adorned with golden fretwork. "This Kabruk lives in even greater splendor than Vatlek," Sinbad said.

Plazzo nodded. "Indeed. Kabruk enjoys every luxury save one—his freedom. Come. Kabruk is waiting."

"He knows we are here?"

"As a spider knows when a dragonfly enters his web—or another spider."

They neared a doorway, and Sinbad heard the sound of sweet voices. He looked in and saw a seraglio beyond a Sultan's dream. A score or more of the most beautiful women lounged on divans and mounds of satin cushions. They beckoned to him, and their song swirled in his ears, pushing away all cares, all woes, all thoughts of his quest.

One of them rose and came forward, arms outstretched. Her perfect breasts swayed to the hypnotic music of her sister's voices. Sinbad inhaled her fragrant perfume. She beckoned to him to enter, and he raised his foot to step through the doorway.

"Halt." Plazzo's word caught Sinbad like a hand at the nape of his neck. The sorcerer waved his hand, and what were the temptress's legs became serpentine coils. The beautiful face twisted into a look of rage, and a forked tongue flicked between her lips as she hissed at Plazzo.

"Lamias," Plazzo said. "Serpent women. Another trap for the unwary."

Sinbad shook his head to clear it.

"If Kabruk knows that we are here, why does he not send a horde of his minions, or a great ball of lightning, or some other terrible thing to stop us?"

"He could destroy us outright, but he has been here for so long, that boredom has become his curse. It amuses him to see how far we will come. He is testing us to determine our worthiness of his presence. Had I let you enter the seraglio, the lamias would have gorged themselves on your flesh and your blood. Or perhaps, if the ring protected you from their fangs, they would have simply wound you in a cocoon of bliss until you finally wasted away."

"And had I not pulled you away, you would have been buried under the dead-fall. But if we are to steal Vashwal's statue, how can we if Kabruk knows our intent?"

"He plays cat to our mouse, or so he thinks, but tables may turn. Theft is a crime of opportunity. With your skills and mine and Fortune's smile, that opportunity will present itself."

They passed other rooms offering treasures unimagined, rich banquets of exotic foods, barrels of wine, but wiser now, at first glance, Sinbad turned his face away from all temptations.

At the corridor's end, an open archway led into a room whose vaulted ceiling disappeared into darkness. Bare walls and a polished floor enclosed a dais, and on it, in a throne carved from a single block of onyx, sat the sorcerer Kabruk.

Sinbad was surprised at the wizard's youthful appearance. He looked to be barely past the threshold of adulthood; a full head of dark hair framed a seamless face, but in his eyes, Sinbad saw the canny wisdom of an aged man. Kabruk wore a purple robe of rich weave that draped all but his head and his hands, which he held, fingers interlaced in his lap. He smiled, the smile a tiger might bestow upon a kid.

"Welcome, Vatlek."

"Vatlek?" Sinbad whirled to stare at his companion, who rose in stature so that his feet were revealed to have no webbing between their toes. Horns retreated, and Vatlek's features replaced Plazzo's. Sinbad cursed under his breath at the deception.

"My greetings to you, Kabruk." Vatlek nodded to their host, and Kabruk returned the nod, the acknowledgment of equals.

"You have brought a friend."

"I have. His name is—"

"Sinbad," Kabruk interrupted. The Captain felt a thrill of dread wash over him, knowing the power a name can hold for a sorcerer

"I have heard tales of the renowned sea captain and his many exploits. It is a privilege to meet you face-to-face, Sinbad. I make so few new acquaintances. As Vatlek has no doubt told you, I never leave this place."

Sinbad wanted dearly to take Vatlek's head from his shoulders, but without the wizard's help, he could never find his way out of Kabruk's palace or back to his ship.

"I have been expecting you, Vatlek. I am surprised that you have waited so long."

"My father's voice calls to me from beyond the grave."

"If he speaks to you from the nether world, it is to call you a treacherous bastard, ungrateful for all the knowledge that he imparted and for more wealth than ten men could exhaust in a lifetime. He has told me so. He curses your very birth."

Vatlek's eyes widened. "He speaks to you?"

"SINBAD CURSED UNDER HIS BREATH AT THE DECEPTION."

"From time to time." Kabruk smiled, amused. "His *ruh* is locked in jade, but his vision ranges far. He told me that you were coming, and he told me when you arrived on the island."

"But Vashwal has not yet revealed his secrets to you, else you would be free to roam the world and make it your own."

Kabruk smiled and changed the subject. "I am being a terrible host. You surely suffer hunger and thirst after your long trek." He clapped his hands, and a pair of heavy-muscled Nubians clad only in loincloths carried in a table laden with trays of meats, cheeses, fruits and pastries, decanters of wine. One of the men brought a plate to the dais. Kabruk took a pomegranate from it, sliced it with a long, sharp fingernail, and his eyes meeting Sinbad's, sank his teeth deep into the fruit. He chewed slowly, deliberately, savoring the flavor, and measuring Sinbad's reaction. A trickle of juice ran from the corner of his mouth to drip from his chin.

Sinbad's mouth watered at the scent of the food. He had eaten nothing that day, but he feared to even touch it, lest it be another trap.

Ignoring the feast, Vatlek said, "I do not come to eat, Kabruk. I come to claim that which is mine, my father's statue and my legacy."

"Claim all you wish," Kabruk said with a smug grin. "Claiming and possessing are different creatures. You cannot force me to surrender the effigy. You have not the power, nor the knowledge, else you would not be here."

"Nor do you have those things in measure to crush me like an irritating insect."

Kabruk pointed a finger at the pair and mouthed a word. Fire shot from his fingertip in a stream toward them. Vatlek spoke, and as Sinbad watched in wonder, the fire washed over and around them as if they were in a protective globe of glass. As abruptly as the fire appeared, it vanished.

Vatlek gestured with his left hand, and a flagstone the size of a man's head detached itself from the floor and spun end over end at the dais. Kabruk raised a hand, and the stone stopped short in mid-air. It hung there for a moment, then Kabruk lowered his hand, and the stone clattered to the floor.

"Neither of us can harm the other, Vatlek, our powers being equal. But I have the upper hand. I have the statue."

"And can do nothing with it."

"Nor could you."

"True until now," Vatlek said, "but together—"

"Together? If we pool our powers and succeed, then what?"

"We share."

Kabruk snorted. "Share. We would share like two pigs at a trough, or two lions at the corpse of a gazelle. The faster jaws get the greater sustenance."

"Then what do you propose?"

"A contest."

"We already know that neither of us can best the other."

"Not you and I. Your man and mine. Philoctes!"

From a curtain behind the dais, a giant stepped, a full head taller than Sinbad. Philoctes enjoyed the shape of statues of Herakles Sinbad had seen in Greece, corded arms and legs like pillars. He wore a brazen breastplate, a helmet that shielded his face, and a copper-scaled girdle around his hips. A sword as long as his arm hung in a scabbard from his belt.

"Let the two fight. Should Sinbad be the victor, you may have the statue. Should Philoctes win, I keep it."

Vatlek shook his head. "Not until I see it before my eyes."

"You do not trust my word?"

"No more than you trust mine."

"Very well." Kabruk clapped his hands, and the Nubians brought out Vashwal's likeness, carrying it with great care, as it were made of eggshell. They set it beside Kabruk's throne. "Say hello to your father, Vatlek."

The jade image was perfect in its form, portraying a man old in years but not in might. He stood erect, arms stiff at his sides. His countenance bore a look of wrath, and Sinbad had to tear his eyes away from its frightful gaze.

Vatlek stood before the statue, and Sinbad saw its brows knit, and its lip raise to show its teeth. One look at Vatlek's expression, and Sinbad knew beyond doubt that this was the object of their quest.

In spite of himself, fear washed across Vatlek's face at the sight. He quickly recovered his composure and said, "Until one or the other calls 'hold'?"

Kabruk shook his head. "Until one or the other lies dead on the floor."

Philoctes drew his sword from its scabbard with a slow grating of metal. Whetstones in the scabbard sharpened the blade every time it moved in or out.

"Your life and mine," Kabruk said over Sinbad's shoulder, "and those of your shipmates." For the first time since the quest began, the confidence was gone from the wizard's voice, replaced with uncertainty. Sinbad looked to the emerald pulsing on his finger and wondered whether it would still protect him in Kabruk's court.

Philoctes slashed at the air in a looping sweep, and at five paces, Sinbad felt the breath of the sword. Philoctes laughed, a deep rumble in his chest. "Prepare to die, seadog." The giant wrapped his hand around the blade of his sword and squeezed it. He opened his palm and it dripped blood on the flagstone. The message was clear: Philoctes had no fear of bleeding.

Sinbad drew his scimitar with one hand, and Grachene with the other. He looked to the scimitar's blade and saw the wavy pattern of the Damascus steel writhe like a living thing. His eyes met Vatlek's, and the sorcerer gave an almost imperceptible nod.

The combatants circled each other, looking for advantage. With a snarl like a panther Philoctes rushed at Sinbad and swept his sword low. Sinbad sprang into the air, pulling his knees to his chest as the sword hissed through the air, scarcely a span below his feet. The ring might protect him, but Sinbad was loath to test it. His feet scarcely touched the floor when Philoctes took a backhanded swipe that made Sinbad snap his head back as the sword's tip flashed past his nose.

He countered with a thrust upward at Philoctes' throat, but the giant beat Sinbad's blade down. Sparks flew. Had it been fashioned of lesser steel, the scimitar would have shattered in Sinbad's hand. A draw cut from Grachene opened a long slit in Philoctes' forearm. Blood wealed from the wound, but Philoctes paid it no heed. He trod forward, sweeping his blade in a figure eight and driving Sinbad backward.

He swung his sword at Philoctes' head, but rather than dodge the strike, Philoctes simply laughed. The blade struck the helmet, and a shock ran up Sinbad's arm, almost making him let go of the handle. Striking Philoctes' charmed helmet was like striking a granite boulder.

The wall was close behind him. Before his opponent could trap him against it, Sinbad dove between Philoctes' legs, rolling as he did, and delivering a kick to the giant's groin. This time, Philoctes roared in pain. Sinbad sprang to his feet and thrust at Philoctes' back, but despite his pain, the giant twisted his torso with unexpected speed, avoiding the blade. He brought the edge of his sword down on to the top of Sinbad's head in a cut that should have split it like a melon, but the ring protected him. He felt no pain, but the force of the blow sent him sprawling.

Philoctes raised his sword over his head with both hands and brought it down full force to cleave Sinbad in two, but Sinbad rolled aside, barely dodging the strike that shattered the stone of the floor.

Sinbad made a side-wise slash at Philoctes' stomach below his breastplate, but once again, the giant dodged the Captain's edge. Sinbad's chest heaved, but Philoctes seemed to barely breathe. Sinbad ran out of his reach to a corner of the room and crouched. Philoctes laughed. "So the great Sinbad runs like a little girl."

"And lives to fight another day." The last words left Sinbad's mouth as he threw his scimitar sidearm, spinning it through the air across the room to slice above Philoctes' breastplate and under his helmet to cleanly take his head from his neck.

Philoctes fell forward with a crash of armor on the stones, his eyes staring at his corpse as his life poured out onto the floor.

Kabruk stared speechless at his champion's lifeless body.

"Sinbad has won, Kabruk," Vatlek said. "I will take the statue now."

Kabruk took another bite of his pomegranate. He chewed thoughtfully for a moment, then his head whipped around to Sinbad, a look of hatred on his face. He spat the pomegranate seeds, which flew at Sinbad like stones from a sling. Sinbad grabbed a tray from the table and held it in front of him as the seeds bounced from it.

Kabruk snarled in anger. "You will take nothing."

"Scoundrel. I should have known you would not honor your word."

"You deserve no honor," Kabruk shot back. His lips moved, and a crackling, vibrating ball of energy so bright that Sinbad had to shield his eyes appeared between the wizards. It swelled until taller than a man, and Kabruk pushed outward with his palms. The sphere began moving across the floor toward Vatlek, who raised his hands likewise. The sorcerers mouthed spell upon spell, pushing the blazing sphere back and forth at each other across the floor, rays of light shooting from their fingertips.

Sinbad looked to the dais and saw that the eyes of Vashwal's statue were fixed upon him. The jade lips moved, and Sinbad heard words without his ears. With no will of his own he clutched Grachene in both hands and ran at the dais. Kabruk was too engaged to stop him, and Sinbad plunged Persephone's gift into the jade, shattering it into myriad fragments.

As he watched in wonderment, the pieces reassembled, not as a statue, but as a shadowy vision of a man, Vashwal's *ruh*.

Vatlek and Kabruk stared in horror as Vashwal raised his hands and uttered an incantation. His voice was not as a man's but like the rush of a great wind. The glowing sphere grew and expanded until it engulfed Vatlek and Kabruk alike. Inside its light, Sinbad saw the wizards quiver with the humming vibration. He watched in fascination as skin and flesh of both shook from their bones to lie like a heap of discarded clothing at their feet. Eyeballs dropped from their screaming skulls, and their skeletons collapsed in a pile on the floor.

The sphere vanished, and the emerald ring slipped from Sinbad's finger and clattered on the flagstones. Sinbad held his breath as Vashwal turned toward him. The voice inside his head spoke once more. "I leave no debts behind me. Return to your ship and leave this place."

"I—I do not know the way. Sorcery brought me here."

Vashwal nodded once, his lips moved, and Sinbad felt himself lifted spinning into air and thrust into blackness.

The grey dawn slowly brought shapes to the jungle from the night's blackness, gently turning them into trees, vines, ferns, like the vision of a man waking from sleep. But none of Sinbad's crew had slept. It was the third dawn, and all were waiting, hoping for their captain's return.

They stared through the portal in the hedgerow they had labored to keep open as the vines slithered across the ground to twist around each other and fill the gap. Their eyes ached to see their captain, but he had not come.

"I say we stay." Ralf folded his arms.

"The Captain's orders were explicit," Henri said. "We are already a night overlong. This is the third sunrise. We should to go to the beach, ready the long boat, and wait."

Ralf looked overhead through the treetops into the grey-misted sky. "I see no sun."

"Do not play the fool, Ralf." Fathi's nostrils flared. You know full well the Captain's intention. You would defy his last order?"

"His thoughts were not for himself but for the safety of his crew and his ship," Henri added.

"Go if you like, but I stand here. I—"

Jafari raised a hand. "Sh! Listen. What is that sound?"

A low whistling filled the air around them, growing louder by the second. All stared through the gap, knowing it could come from nowhere else. One second they saw nothing. The next, they saw Sinbad fall from the sky to land with a thump on the grassy lea.

Sinbad shook his head, dazed. Vashwal's sorcery had delivered him to his companions. He could see them through the tunnel through the wall of grey vines.

"Captain! Captain!" their voices called.

Sinbad stepped toward the opening, but with speed unimagined, the vines shot across the gap like striking cobras to weave the hedgerow shut.

Ralf roared with rage and hacked at the fresh vines. The others joined him but as quickly as they cut a ropy strand away, two more replaced it. In a moment, the portal was closed.

Sinbad looked back to Kabruk's stronghold and saw its walls shudder and collapse inward, disappearing into a great hole in the ground. As he watched in horror, the swirling funnel expanded, swallowing all things around it. Soon, it would be at his heels.

Ralf, Henri, and Jafari renewed their attack with fury, but they could not cut quickly enough as the snaking vines coiled around their arms and legs.

"That does no good," Henri said. "Stand clear." He struck flint to steel and in a moment, a crackling fire rose in the vines. It spread, hot and fast as the vines twisted to escape the flames, but they had done their work too well. They could not untangle themselves quickly enough, and soon the gap was open once again, but ringed with fire.

Sinbad wrapped his arms around his head and charged through the blazing vines. He stumbled halfway through, but strong hands seized his arms. Ralf and Jafari pulled him through to the other side.

"Fathi?" Sinbad said, looking around.

Henri shook his head and said, "The wizard?"

"Gone," Sinbad said, slapping out sparks on his clothing. "We must hurry. The island is collapsing within itself. Run!"

The men needed no second urging.

The Blue Nymph bobbed at anchor, like a restful steed pawing at the ground, tethered to a post. Omar watched as the rim of the sun edged over the horizon, turning the sky crimson. He called up to Haroun. "Any sign?"

"None," the watchman replied.

"Beware you do not fall asleep."

"I have not slept these three nights, Omar, but I doubt I could if struck with a club."

Sinbad's orders were clear: sail away if he and his crew did not return in the time given. Omar could wait a little longer, but he felt he had waited long enough.

"Raise the anchor!"

"What course, Omar?" Called Hammaz at the helm.

"South. Back to the island."

Tishmi was first to feel the earth shake. "Do you feel that, Rafi?"

Rafi frowned and put his palm to the ground. His eyes shifted from side to side." An earthquake? A volcano?"

"It grows stronger. Listen!"

From inside the island a rumbling came that grew with every breath.

"We should untie the boat," Rafi looked to the trees where the long boat was tied with two lines to a thick bole.

"We have no sign of the Captain," Tishmi said.

"We should be ready to launch when he comes." He looked warily to the beach as the black sand began to dance.

Two sweeps of Tishmi's sword, and the ropes were severed. She and Rafi were struggling to drag the long boat to the water's edge when Sinbad and his companions burst from the jungle.

"Launch the boat," Sinbad shouted. "The island is caving in!"

In moments, the long boat was in the water and crew were at the oars, Sinbad pulling in Fathi's place. "Row for your lives!" As he looked back to the island, he saw the jungle trees tumbling inward as the funnel expanded. They cleared the cove and were half a league to sea when the funnel's edge reached the beach. The black sand slid into the hole like rice from a scoop. And then, as Sinbad watched in horror, the sea began to pour in after.

The Blue Nymph sped southward at full sail, Omar steering the ship. Where was the island? Surely they should have reached it by this time. "Haroun," he called to the lookout. "Any sign?"

"None, Omar. I cannot yet see it. I see only—wait!" Haroun shaded his brow with a hand. "The long boat, rowing this way."

"My Blue Lady," Omar said to the ship, "put on all your speed."

In the long boat, Sinbad felt the drag on the oars. The sea rushing into the vortex left by the disappearing island was pulling against them, tugging the long boat backward toward the swirling maw. He did not need to tell the crew to pull harder. Strain showed on every face as they rowed against the powerful tide.

Jafari looked over his shoulder and cried out, "Sails! The Blue Nymph!"

Without the ring's protection, he was now vulnerable, and so was the ship. Sinbad looked back and saw her approaching, but would she reach them soon enough?

At the top of the mast, Haroun stared past the long boat and saw the swirling whirlpool swallowing the sea. "Omar! Behind them, a whirlpool pulling them back!"

Not only did the sucking hole in the ocean jeopardize the long boat, it could pull the Blue Nymph in with it. Omar had to not only rescue Sinbad and his shipmates but then escape its draw. He worked the helm, tacking and jibing to pull every ounce of speed he could from the wind in the sails. From the bridge, he could now see the long boat, a speck on the horizon. With luck they would succeed. "Mother Ocean," he whispered, "Save us all."

The crew's effort was valiant, but as hard as they rowed, the edge of the vortex edged slowly closer, as if they were holding the boat in place as the gaping mouth neared to swallow them. They could hear it now, a sound like a mammoth waterfall filling their ears.

Around him, Sinbad heard prayers in different languages to different gods. The Blue Nymph was closing on them but so was spinning death. He could feel it now; the long boat was slowly slipping backward.

Omar realized that if he continued on his course, he might reach the long boat and save his shipmates, but a hands-breadth of miscalculation could sail the Blue Nymph into the whirlpool's grasp. They were thirty fathoms away now, with the vortex's edge close behind. If he could only get close enough to throw them a line, the Blue Nymph might win the tug-of-war and pull them clear.

It was clear to Sinbad that he and his party were losing the contest. The roaring in his ears was so loud that he barely heard Jafari's voice. "Captain, I have an idea."

A coil of rope lay in the bow of the long boat. Jafari tied it through the ring at his harpoon's tail. The Blue Nymph was twenty fathoms away now. Sinbad could see the crew in the rigging.

"Great Damballah, guide my arm," Jafari said as he stood in the boat and hurled his harpoon. It flew straight and true, arcing through the air over the rail for its barbed tip to wedge in the ship's deck, bringing the rope with it.

"Quickly, lash that rope to the mast," Omar shouted. He pulled hard to port and swung the Blue Nymph's stern to the great sucking hole. The wind filled the blue sails, and for a moment Omar felt the ship slide backward, but the sails caught, and he could feel her not only move forward, but pick up speed.

Sinbad could see over the edge of the funnel now, its glassy green wall spinning downward. Jafari's harpoon had reached the ship, but was it soon enough to save them? His lungs ached as he pulled at his oar, determined to not give up. He would fight for every breath until the end.

He blinked and looked again. The lip of the whirlpool was receding. The Blue Nymph was pulling them away from certain death. Cries of exultation rang from the long boat and the ship alike as the Blue Nymph towed Sinbad and his companions further to sea. Crewmen pulled in the line hand over hand and soon, the long boat was raised, and all were safe aboard.

"That was as close as could be," Omar said.

"Close, but it did not touch." Sinbad clapped his friend on the shoulder. He looked back toward the vortex and shuddered at the thought of what might have been.

"Something is happening," Haroun cried. From his perch, he saw what the others could not. The funnel was finally full. As the crew watched in amazement, a column of water shot into the sky like a green fountain, splashed down again, and the sea was calm. It sent a tall wave in all directions, slapping the mermaid and shoving the Blue Nymph forward.

"Sorcery." Omar spat. "If ever you cross paths with a wizard again, find yourself a new mate, eh?" The look on his Captain's face cut Omar's laughter short. "What troubles you, Sinbad?"

Sinbad looked to his empty finger. "Am I truly free of Vatlek's hold? I must know. Are there pomegranates yet in our stores?"

"I will send a man to look."

In a moment, Omar held out the blood red fruit to Sinbad.

Sinbad hesitated, took a breath, then quickly before changing his mind plucked the pomegranate from Omar's palm, and bit into the fruit. The juice ran down his chin. He chewed slowly, savoring the mix of tart and sweet. Nothing happened. Sinbad decided that no fruit would ever taste better again.

Omar nodded. "Now, Sinbad, that you are your own master once again, what course shall I set?"

Sinbad pondered the question for a moment then said, "What other?" His eyes cast eastward. "To the edge of the Earth."

THE END

The Challenge

It's always a challenge to write a story starring someone else's character. I try my best to be true to the original portrayal, but it's even more of a challenge doing the job with a long-established cultural icon from the *Thousand and One Arabian Nights.*

Since Sinbad is pretty well locked in as a character, that left plotting as the most open avenue for creativity. Since Sinbad stories are fantasy fare, I had fun subjecting him and his companions to all sorts of bizarre perils. To prepare for the task, I not only studied the character bible but read folktales and fairy tales to get the feel of their formal language structure in both narrative and dialog.

The result, I hope, is an entertaining story, true to the tradition of the *Arabian Nights.*

FRED ADAMS JR - is a retired Penn State English Instructor who splits his time between writing pulp fiction and performing as Cedric the Butler on the Internet TV show Terror Night Theatre (terrornighttheatre.com). His Airship 27 books include the *Hitwolf* series, the C.O. Jones series, the Sam Dunne mysteries, the Smith Brothers mysteries, the Ike Mars mysteries, the *Six Gun Terrors* series, and contributions to numerous anthologies. His most recent work is *Dan Fowler G-Man Volume Five.* Visit Fred's website at http://drphreddee.com/author

www.ingramcontent.com/pod-product-compliance
Lightning Source LLC
LaVergne TN
LVHW010924110826
845149LV00013B/2467

* 9 7 8 1 9 6 9 2 8 5 1 5 8 *